GOOD LOSERS

R. LLOYD HALL

PRESS®
A DIVISION OF THOMAS NELSON
& ZONDERVAN

WestBow Press books may be ordered through booksellers or by contacting:

WestBow Press
A Division of Thomas Nelson & Zondervan
1663 Liberty Drive
Bloomington, IN 47403
www.westbowpress.com
844-714-3454

Because of the dynamic nature of the Internet, any web addresses or
links contained in this book may have changed since publication and
may no longer be valid. The views expressed in this work are solely those
of the author and do not necessarily reflect the views of the publisher,
and the publisher hereby disclaims any responsibility for them.

Any people depicted in stock imagery provided by Getty Images are
models, and such images are being used for illustrative purposes only.
Certain stock imagery © Getty Images.

ISBN: 979-8-3850-2647-0 (sc)
ISBN: 979-8-3850-2646-3 (e)

Library of Congress Control Number: 2024910914

Print information available on the last page.

WestBow Press rev. date: 06/26/2024

I hereby give all rights to the artwork I have created for the book "Good Losers" to the author, R. Lloyd Hall. The artwork consists of nine images.

Jane K. Schreiner

Jane Schreiner

SPECIAL THANKS

A special thank you to our daughter, Heather Abbring, and her daughter, Dana Abbring, for proof-reading the book and making a lot of suggestions and corrections.

Also, a special thanks to our daughter, Heidi Marshall, for proof-reading the book and for all her help with technical matters and formatting.

Finally, a special thanks to Author Jerry Slauter. I met Jerry at a Christian Fellowship Fest a few years ago. He wrote two period books and it took him quite a few years to finish the first one. Jerry encouraged me to finish this book which I had started some 40 years ago.

CONTENTS

CHAPTER 1
TRADITIONS

A small gray-haired lady turned on the old portable radio, reached down into her laundry basket, pulled out a light gray blouse, and set it on the ironing board.

"And in local sports..." the announcer intoned, "Coach Henry Gayton comes out of retirement today to take over as head coach of Coral High School's football team, the Lancers."

"Everyone is still wondering why Coach Gayton, who retired five years ago after a tremendously successful thirty-five-year coaching career at Vermillion University that included several national championships, would come back to take a one-year unpaid coaching position at Coral High School. Coral, a small rural high school that has only existed for five years, has never won - or even tied - a single football game. Last year they only scored three touchdowns all year and their closest loss had a score of 28-6. The team's first practice starts at Lancer Field this morning at 9:00 a.m. where a record number of players are expected to turn out."

Mrs. Farnsworth looked up from her ironing and glanced out her window which overlooked the Coral High School football field. It was still early but most of the players had already arrived. "What a bunch of losers!" she muttered. "They can't win a single game in five whole years. Nothing but losers!"

Down on the field Coach Gayton and his assistants were trying to get forty or so guys organized and assessing exactly what they had to work with. Paul Horn, a thin young man with thick glasses who looked more like a jockey or a marathon runner than anybody remotely connected with football, was the offensive coordinator and the only one of the three coaches who had been with the team last year. Paul was the first to speak. "Coach, do you want the good news first?"

Coach Gayton smiled slightly. "I could use a little good news right now. Give me all you can spare!"

"Well, we've got 48 guys trying out for the team!"

"Go on, I hope there's more."

"Sorry, that's about all the GOOD news," said Paul. He'd been hoping the coach would be more impressed. "Last year we started with about thirty and, with injuries and guys quitting and all, we ended up with only twenty-three."

"Well, about a dozen or so LOOK like football players and the rest look more like candidates for the golf team or chess team," the coach observed wryly.

"You've got to remember that this is a small-town high school, not a big-time university like you're used to."

"I guess you're right," sighed the coach. "Any of these guys play last year and, if so, what positions and how well?"

"See that kid in the orange tee shirt? He was our back-up quarterback last year. His name is Kenny Turner. He played in three games, threw ten passes, completed two, and had three intercepted. Ralph Jackson, the one in the torn blue jeans, played tight end and linebacker. He caught nine or ten passes on offense and plays pretty good defense. And the red-haired kid next to him is Neal Granger. Naturally everybody calls him 'Red.' I guess there was a famous player a long time ago named Red Granger. Anyway, he was our top running back last year. He's fairly small but he's got good speed. He's real quick getting to the hole. Unfortunately, there were hardly any holes for him to get to. He did score two of our three touchdowns and also plays a pretty good cornerback on defense."

"How about the really big guy over there, the one with the ridiculous looking straw hat? If he can move AT ALL, it will make my day!" the coach said hopefully.

"Well, I really did save the best for last," Paul replied with all the enthusiasm he could muster. "That's Dexter Middleton and, if he was with any other team last year, he would have been All Conference or even All State at both offensive and defensive tackle. Unfortunately, as soon as other teams found out how good he was, they triple teamed him on every play. He still led the team in tackles. He IS a player and, if the team has a leader, he's probably it."

"Maybe there are some things to build on then," said Coach Gayton, somewhat encouraged. "How about kickers? Who punts and can anybody kick extra points...or at least kick off?"

"I don't know. The guy who kicked last year missed all three extra points, had his only two field goal tries blocked, averaged only 21 yards on kickoffs and not much better on punts. Besides, he graduated. We do have a couple of guys from the soccer team trying out as place kickers, but nobody really looks like a punter."

"Well, if we can't pass and we can't catch, we can't kick and we can't cover, and we can't block and we can't tackle, we can't win. So, we've got a LOT of work to do! So let's get started..." Coach decided a short motivational speech might help--it definitely couldn't hurt, and in his mind, he needed a little motivation himself.

"Gentlemen, gather around and listen up!"

The coach introduced himself and his small staff: the aforementioned offensive coordinator Paul Horn, and Thad Holloway, the defensive coordinator and now rather overweight former high school lineman who had never done any coaching before. The only others were student assistants. Coach Gayton then talked briefly about football being a lot like life, how it's a team game, and the importance of discipline. He looked out at the 48 young men.

His thoughts flashed back to his many years at Vermillion. There he always had special greetings for each player on the first day of practice. But there he had already known each player - either because he had been involved in recruiting them out of high school or because they had been with the team the year before. Here, in spite of Paul's descriptions of some of them, he really knew no one. He had no idea what they were like or what, if any, talents they had. Figuring that out had to be the starting point. Vermillion University had a long and proud football tradition. Coral High School had gone five full years, 45 games, without a single win. Not the kind of tradition a coach can refer to. Actually, the kind of tradition you want the players to forget.

He finished his brief talk with, "and today we start a new... WINNING tradition here at Coral High School. And with hard work...and TEAM work, we, YOU, WILL WIN!"

He hoped he sounded more confident than he felt.

The coach had the players break up into groups - linemen in one group, backs and receivers in another and potential kickers and holders in a third. Offense and defense would come later, since many if not most would play both ways. He put Thad Holloway in charge of the linemen, Paul Horn in charge of backs and receivers, and he took the kickers and holders for now. Although few of the players started off in that group, he wanted to work with that area first. They all started with warm-up exercises, then conditioning drills. It was going to be a fairly hot day; it was best to get the harder exercises out of the way early. Then there was timed running to get some idea about speed, strength, and agility, which he was afraid this team would have in rather short supply.

Despite these initial fears, he was happy to find there was a great deal of enthusiasm, even in spite of all the hard, tedious work. That was a good sign.

One thin, wiry young man seemed especially lost out on the

field. Coach walked over to him. "What is your name, son?" he asked.

"Eldon, sir!" he replied, obviously surprised and a bit dismayed that the coach even noticed him and not too sure he hadn't already done something wrong. "Eldon Spicer."

The young man stood a little over six feet tall and weighed about 145 pounds. He looked like if you hit him very hard, he would shatter into little pieces. "How would you like to be our holder, at least for today? inquired Coach Gayton.

"Sure!" Eldon responded, extremely relieved that he hadn't really messed up, at least not yet. Coach looked around for a long snapper candidate. After a little searching he found one of the farm boys, Bailey Grant, who at least looked like he could both snap the ball far enough and possibly block somebody afterward. He was about 5'10", maybe 200 pounds, and muscular. Coach Gayton set up the soccer kickers with tees in front of the goal posts and had them practice kicking. Then he went to work with Eldon and Bailey.

First, he had Bailey snap the ball and Eldon catch it while kneeling on the turf. When the two of them got that down fairly well, he had Eldon actually place the ball on the grass. Coach pointed out the proper position of the ball and how to spin the ball quickly so the laces face forward. After the two of them got comfortable with that, Coach left them alone to keep practicing.

Then he went to check on his kickers. Coach Gayton had never actually worked with kickers before. Assistants had always handled that at Vermillion; that had always been their job, not his. But he had seen enough through the years to know the basics. However, teaching a couple of guys from the soccer team, used to kicking a round ball, how to kick a football—THAT he wasn't sure about. And with these two guys, he began to wonder if the soccer team had ever won a game, either.

As practice was winding down, Coach had seen enough of his potential kicking game. The long snapper and holder were the least of his problems. An extra point, from a line of scrimmage of the three yard line, is actually the same as a 20 yard field goal. Maybe three or four yards beyond that was about as far as either of his kickers could kick with any degree of accuracy. And they were still pretty slow getting the kicks off. That, coupled with pretty much a one-man offensive line, could be disastrous. And their punts, when they didn't fumble the snap, could barely make it past the line of scrimmage and had almost no hang time.

Maybe they could try rugby style kicking. But that could wait until another day.

The already warm air was quickly getting downright hot, not to mention humid, so Coach had the players run a fifty-yard dash and the assistants timed and recorded each one, along with their height and weight. Then he had the players run a few laps around the field and sent them to the showers. The coaches all headed for the air-conditioned office to compare notes and first day observations. Coach Gayton took a quick look at Thad's notes on the linemen candidates and noted that Dexter Middleton stood 6'2" and weighed 305 pounds. His running times weren't bad, either. If he was really as good as Paul said he was, maybe there was a block to build around. The problem was that he outweighed everyone else on the team by almost 100 pounds. There would be nobody to have him practice against to even give him any real exercise. The real problem was at quarterback. Kenny Turner couldn't throw a spiral if his life depended on it. Any pass over ten or fifteen yards downfield was so wobbly it died quickly and was also pretty hard to catch. If that couldn't be improved, defenses could play everybody up close to the line of scrimage and make running the ball really difficult.

At Vermillion, Coach had always been known as an innovator with wide open offenses, long passes, reverses, and a long string of outstanding quarterbacks and wide receivers. He had seen absolutely nothing that looked like that type of offense here. The three coaches worked on some ideas for a basic offense and a basic defense for several hours. They sent out for some food, worked through lunch and late into the afternoon. Finally, very tired and still not too sure about any of this, Coach decided to call it a day.

CHAPTER 2
A PASSING GLANCE

After retiring, Coach and his wife, Kelly, had bought a house in a new subdivision on the very outskirts of town. Acorn Lakes Estates bordered on the Acorn Lakes Country Club, a first-class private golf course. His wife's parents lived within a few miles of their house, which was convenient. Coach's mother lived with them. It was a huge home, far more than they really needed for just the three of them, but their grown children visited them occasionally and then, the extra rooms came in handy.

For the last several years Coach had spent many hours working on his golf game. And they had traveled. Eventually he realized that he missed the excitement of the game and working with young men and helping them, not just with football, but with life. When he found out that the Coral football coach had quit and taken a teaching job in another state just a couple of weeks before Fall football practice was supposed to start, he jumped at the chance.

Now he realized this was going to be a real challenge. One thing for sure, it wasn't going to be boring. Hopefully, they wouldn't go 0-9 again. He might have been out of coaching for five years, but he didn't think he was out of touch. On the other hand, Coach Gayton was now 67 years old and would be trying to coach kids as young as fifteen. He decided that respect would be a two way street. He would have to earn their respect through his coaching skills and experience. But they would also have to earn his respect, at least by their hard work, if not their record.

He stopped quickly at the house and grabbed his clubs and took off again for the golf course. He had enough time to at least get in a quick nine holes before before dark. His wife wasn't home anyway so he left a note. Golf usually, depending on how he was playing, was relaxing and took his mind off everything else, which right now would be a good thing. And he had a pretty good round, even sinking a couple of long putts. As he finished, it was almost dusk.

As he was driving home he passed another house in the same subdivision. Coach noticed it because it was a brand new house and until now it had been unoccupied. As he passed by he saw a football flying through the air. Even from a distance he could see the ball had a nice, tight spiral as it arced gracefully between two shadowy figures in a large back yard. He made a mental note for future reference. It was a long shot. The guys could be grown men. Or they could be students at one of the nearby private schools. But if someone could throw like that—it would definitely be worth checking.

For the next several days the coaches wrestled with settling on some kind of offense and defense. For the defense, Coach Gayton preferred a 4-3 with Dexter and Bailey Grant as two of the four linemen. But if he put Dexter in the middle, that might make it easier to double- or triple-team him. And if he put Dexter on the outside, it would make it a lot easier to run to the opposite side. And on offense, with the exception of Dexter, no one on the line looked capable of really blocking well. That might dictate a lot of misdirection and trap blocks, since it was painfully obvious their quarterback couldn't throw the ball very far downfield. They could spread the receivers, but using them as decoys would never fool anyone for very long. They HAD to develop some kind of passing game or they might not even score three touchdowns this year. Ralph Jackson looked like a fairly respectable tight end. He had reasonable speed and could both get open and catch the ball. At about 6' 1" and 185 pounds, he was pretty small for a tight end but was a fairly good-sized high school linebacker. Otherwise, it seemed like the few guys that were fairly fast couldn't catch the ball and the guys that could catch were slow and could rarely get open. And that was against their own defense... which wasn't that fast in the first place.

At one point Coach Gayton asked Dexter if he knew anyone else at Coral that might help in the line. "You know, big and strong, like you?"

"There is one guy," said Dexter, "but he's kind of lazy and doesn't like football."

"Could you at least talk to him?" Coach asked. "If we don't get you some help in the line, you're going to have to do it almost all by yourself. Just see if you can get him to come to my office and I'll give it a shot."

"His name is Lindell Patterson and he's about 5' 11" and probably 230 or 235 pounds," said Dexter. "He was on the wrestling team last year as a heavyweight but quit when they wanted him to do some work in the weight room. I'll give it a try. He's pretty much of a Total Otis, though."

"Okay, I'll bite." said Coach. "What exactly is a Total Otis?"

"Well, Otis is a company that makes elevators. Their slogan is 'You can count on us to let you down.'" said Dexter.

"So a 'Total Otis' is someone you can count on to let you down?"

"You got it, Coach," laughed Dexter. "But I WILL try."

The next day, sure enough, Lindell Patterson did stop by the coach's office. He was around 235 pounds all right, but very little of that 235 pounds was muscle. Coach almost chuckled. At Vermillion they had referred to guys shaped like that as guys who could do the nine yard dash in a hundred seconds flat. But he at least had the weight to do some serious blocking if he was willing to work and build up some strength. After what Dexter had said, that was no sure thing. Coach told "Lindy" (as the young man preferred to be called) that the team could use a player of his size if he was willing to work hard, build up his strength and endurance, and learn how to block and tackle. Finally Coach asked if he was willing to make that commitment. A long silence followed. He could see that Lindy wasn't real excited about working that hard.

Eventually Lindy said, "I THINK I'd like to try it. Can I discuss it with my folks and let you know tomorrow?"

Coach remembered Dexter's comments about Lindy but, as he looked at the potential lineman standing in front of him he said "You and Dexter could make quite a pair. By all means! If you want to join the team, your parents have to fill out some paperwork and you need a physical exam, so stop back tomorrow and let me know. I'll have everything ready so if your answer is "yes," we can start right away." Coach showed Lindy to the door. "I know you can do it if you really want to. But only you can decide that."

Practices were going reasonably well but the first game was only three weeks away now. And the passing game, in particular, was going badly. Even after several weeks of work, Kenny Turner still could not throw a spiral. The ball would come out of his hand fluttering and anything beyond five yards past the line of scrimmage was not only inaccurate but also very hard to catch. Coach had been checking out the house where he had seen the two guys throwing nice, tight spirals every night on his way home from football practice but had not seen anyone there since that night.

Lindy Patterson came to practice the next morning, picked up all the necessary paperwork and headed off for his physical. He at least had some size and, with some hard work, could provide some balance for both the offensive and defensive lines. If he could just hold his own, other teams couldn't double and triple team Dexter. Then Coral's running game and run defense might actually work.

Coral's first game would be an away game against the Borderline Bobcats. Borderline was a mid-sized high school about 25 miles from Coral. They had entered the Cross County Conference a few years before Coral High School was built and their athletic teams, particularly their football teams weren't much more successful than Coral's. However, so far Coral had yet to come close to beating them. The small town was located right on the county line, thus the name. This was one of the games the coaches thought Coral could possibly win. IF they came well prepared and ready to play. And every day after practice, that seemed less and less likely.

The days went by quickly. Lindy Patterson was really trying. But he started in such poor physical condition and his endurance was so lacking that Coach had been very lenient at practice so far. A couple of conditioning drills and he would be totally winded; the question was whether he'd be able to play at all in the first game. And the hot fall weather didn't help. The coaches moved most of practice to early morning before it got too hot and humid.

Finally one day on the way home, Coach spotted a football flying again in the same yard as before. This time he stopped and watched. Not wanting to look suspicious, he parked the car on the side of the road and observed. First he saw those same long, graceful passes arc back and forth. Then he heard several resounding thumps as the two young men kicked the ball to each other. Finally, he had seen enough. If there was even a little sliver of a chance these guys could play for Coral, he had to take it. He got out of his car and walked over to see who these guys were.

CHAPTER 3
LONG SHOTS

Coach approached the yard and found two young African American boys playing catch with a football. He introduced himself. "Guys, I am Coach Henry Gayton, head football coach at Coral High School this year. What school will you be attending?" The two young men explained that they had just moved to Coral and would be attending Coral High starting in just a few weeks. Coach was ecstatic. The older of the two, Wayde Davis, would be a Senior. His brother, Elston Davis, would be a Sophomore. "Would you both be interested in joining our football team?" Coach asked trying to hide his excitement.

After a long pause Wayde spoke up. "WE might like to" he replied. "But our Mom is afraid we'd get seriously hurt. She's always said 'no.' And she's pretty adamant about it."

"Do you think I could talk to her?" asked Coach Gayton, trying to hide his disappointment.

"You can try." said Wayde. She'll be here tomorrow evening. "Dad is here now but he's not the one you have to convince. He works for the Post Office and just got transferred. He's the new Coral Postmaster. We're still kind of moving in. If you can make it at about 6:00 p.m., that should work out well. We'll tell them you're coming."

Coach shook hands with the young men, then walked across the road to his car and headed home. He was certain that these two would really improve the chances of the football team if he could just convince their mother. Either one would be a vast improvement at the quarterback position. On top of that, they could both kick fairly well. Now he had to do some homework.

When he arrived home he went into his den and turned on the computer. Coach was never a computer geek but, through the years, he had reluctantly modernized. Now he owned a smart phone and a tablet, Although he still preferred reading most of the time on the nice, big desktop monitor in his den. He clicked into the "Google" search engine and then typed in "High School Football Injury Statistics."

He hoped to find some encouraging information.

Coach found that 1.5 million boys participate in high school football each year and there were about 1.2 million injuries each year. About 12 boys die each year, four directly from football injuries and eight from indirect causes such as weak hearts, etc. 50 percent of injuries were to lower extremities, 36 percent injuries to knees. 10 to 15 percent of the injuries were concussions. This wasn't exactly what he had hoped to find.

Coach Gayton had been retired for several years. He never had any of his players die or even become paralyzed. But he did know coaches who had such occurences. For them it had been devastating. One had retired. Another had become an alcoholic. If anyone knew the chances of injury, it was the coaches. He had hoped things had changed since he had retired. Newer and better helmets and equipment, better coaching, less contact in practice, and tougher rules against spearing and other, more dangerous hits had certainly reduced injuries through the years. But football is still a contact sport and when bodies collide at high speeds, there will always be the chance of injuries. So all these statistics were in no way going to convince the boys' mother that it was safe to let them play. If anything, they would reinforce her concerns. He turned off the computer. Maybe he could think of some better ideas tomorrow. After a good night's sleep.

The next day went all together too fast and the 6:00 p.m. meeting was quickly approaching. And Coach Gayton still didn't have any really good ideas. As a college assistant and later head coach he had sat in probably thousands of living rooms and a few other places talking to parents and young men about coming to his school. But they were already *players*...he didn't have to convince them to *play*, just to come and play for Vermillion University. And as coach, he was offering the recruits a full-ride scholarship. Here, Coach was only offering...

Maybe that was the approach he should be using. But exactly what, beside the possibility of getting injured, <u>was</u> he offering? He'd have to think about that. And he didn't have a lot of time.

All too soon, it was a few minutes before 6:00 and he was ringing the doorbell at the Davis home. Wayde answered the door and led him inside. "Good luck!" Wayde half whispered. Mom, Dad, this is Coach Gayton. He's here to talk to you about..."

"We know!" Alicia Davis cut her son off in mid-sentence. "But I think this is a big waste of Coach's time. Football is just too dangerous. Coach, we've been through this with our boys before.'."

Coach thought of the effect these two young men could conceivably have on his otherwise less-than-impressive, to say the least, team. If he was going to lose this "battle" he was going to go down fighting. "Is the chance of getting seriously hurt the only reason you don't want them to play?" asked the coach. If there were other reasons he wanted to know before going any further.

"Yes, but isn't that a good enough reason?" Alicia responded. "I have read about players ending up in wheelchairs, paralyzed for the rest of their lives and others have even died. I don't want to take any chances with our two boys."

Coach did not answer quickly. He could see that Alicia was

sincerely concerned about her boys' safety. Mr. Davis had yet to say anything at all and it was obvious that Alicia was the key. If Coach couldn't convince her, his cause was lost. The pause seemed to last half a forever. Finally Coach spoke. "IF the boys were to play I can't guarantee they wouldn't be hurt. Injuries do happen. According to one set of statistics from a few years ago, about one and-a-half million boys play high school football each year. And there are about 1.2 million injuries each year, most relatively minor. But ten to fifteen percent are concussions. And there are about four deaths directly related to high school football each year with another eight indirectly related, such as weak hearts. So I could point to very small odds, similar to the odds of being struck by lightning or even less than the odds for being killed or injured in a car accident...but the chances are still there and I can't deny that."

"But, let's look at what should happen if you agree to let them play. What does playing football for Coral High School offer for your sons? First, you are all new to town. There are very few better ways to make new friends than to be teammates on a football team. Working hard, together, toward a common goal, the shared experiences, the joy of competition, the camaraderie--these are things that are very hard to find outside of team sports. And, as a possible bonus, if your sons are as good as I think they can be, possible scholarships. I've been retired for a few years but I still have friends and connections from my college coaching years. If they play, and play well, while I can't guarantee anything, I will do my best to find scholarships for them." At this last semi-promise Coach could see Wendell Davis, the boys' father, perk up a bit.

"Did you play high school sports?" inquired the coach, sensing at least a tiny little opening..

Wendell Davis spoke first. "I played basketball, both in high school and then for a junior college team near Atlanta. Then I wrecked my knee and, after surgery, had to give it up."

"And you, Mrs. Davis?" Coach asked.

"I played tennis for a couple of years in high school" admitted

Alicia. "And I did enjoy it, although I wasn't exactly Serena Williams when it came to talent. But tennis, and even basketball aren't nearly as dangerous as football. Do you have any sons?" she asked abruptly.

Coach was somewhat surprised at the question. But he could see exactly where this was going. And he knew he would have to be both honest and sincere. "We have three daughters but no sons." he replied. "They ran cross country and played soccer," he continued. "But I know what you want to ask: if I DID have a son, would I have let him play football?"

Again, there was a long pause. It wasn't a question he had ever really thought about before. And the Davis's decision could very well depend on his answer. "It would be very easy for me to just say 'yes,'" said the coach thoughtfully. "Honestly it's not something that ever came up before. But the answer would have to be a qualified yes. There is no way I could have coached all those young men on my teams if I didn't believe the game was basically safe, though not without dangers. Their parents entrusted them to us, the coaches and staff. They weren't just players, they became our surrogate sons. So yes, if I had a son, and he wanted to play, I would have let him. I would have never pressured him to play, but if he wanted to, I would have let him and even encouraged him. Long ago, I played on the junior varsity team at my high school. I wasn't big enough or strong enough or fast enough to make the varsity team. And I got dinged up and bruised a few times. But I have always treasured my experiences, limited though they were."

There was another long pause. Everyone seemed to be pondering both the questions and the answers. And nobody seemed ready to come up with any more questions. It seemed to be a good time to leave. Coach stood up and said thoughtfully "I can see that this is a really important decision for you, and a whole family decision, at that. Why don't you think about it at least overnight, or even for a day or so, and then let me know what you decide."

One of the first rules of salesmanship is to not let the "buyer" think about it, but rather to push for a decision right now. Coach, based on his many years of college recruiting, knew this was not the prescribed path to success but he also felt that, if he pushed for a decision right now, the answer would be "no." And he had planted several "seeds" that might just take a little time to germinate. At least that is what he told himself as he drove home, and that is what he sincerely hoped..

CHAPTER 4
A PLEASANT SURPRISE

The next morning practice was going fairly well. Kenny Turner was, at least somewhat, beginning to grasp the idea of how to throw an actual spiral, and his arm strength was improving at least marginally. The players were finally getting used to the terminology and what their responsibilities were on any given play. Not that they usually *executed* that responsibility--but they at least remembered what it was. The defense was also starting to work together reasonably well. The coaches had finally agreed on a four-three set-up with Dexter as one tackle, Lindy Patterson (who was finally showing some stamina and strength) as the other tackle. Bailey Grant, (the long snapper for punts and kicks) would be at one defensive end and Allen Greene at 5'10" and 175 lbs. at the other. Wesley Grant, Bailey's younger brother, was the center. He was 5'9" tall and weighed 190. This group looked, at practice anyway, to be a fairly solid defensive line. But that was part of the problem. At practice there were no other players to give them any real challenge. Dexter looked great and Coach had tried to build the rest of the team around him. The first game, coming now in less than two weeks, would show them a lot about how good...or bad...they were.

For defense, at the three linebacker spots were the aforementioned Eldon Spicer and Ralph Jackson, and Herm Milligan at 6' 0" and 150 lbs. The problem was, with the exception of Ralph, the guys who had at least some speed were underweight, (at least for linebackers), and the guys who had some weight were pretty slow.

Holding down the two safety positions were Roger Morrison, who was 6'2" tall but only weighed 160 lbs., and T. C. Fanning, at 5'9" and 185 lbs.

Morrison, whose nickname was Rigor Mortis, given to him by Dexter, was probably the fastest guy on the team. However, he had really small hands. He had the speed to catch up with just about anybody but had a lot of trouble tackling. Definitely a work in progress. If he could actually catch the ball, the coaches would have made him a wide receiver. But in spite of a lot of hard work with the offense, he ended up at left safety and only played defense.

Fanning was a pretty good tackler but not quite fast enough to catch up with anybody with any real speed at all. But he was too good to leave on the bench so he was put in as right safety.

If defense was a bit questionable, offense was even more of a major problem. If your passing game is limited to nothing further than ten yards past the line of scrimmage and the other team's eleven defensive guys can all line up and stay in those ten yards, it is very difficult for even really good offenses to consistently get first downs, let alone scores. And Kenny Turner's range was still about ten yards or so. His occasional spirals were easier to catch, but that was a mixed blessing. While it was easier for the intended receiver to catch, it was also easier to intercept. Quick slant passes, screen passes, and draw plays can work as change-of-pace plays; however, a steady diet of these is a recipe for disaster. The coaches had even tried to get Neil Granger to throw an occasional option pass, but that hadn't worked either. Neil couldn't even throw the ball as far as Kenny, although he did have a better spiral. They had also tried Roger Morrison as an end, putting him in motion and giving him the ball on an end-around play, but he kept dropping the ball. They had tried using Dexter as a running back. That had worked to some degree, but Dexter was much better at opening holes for Granger than he was as a powerful but relatively slow running back. He threw devastating blocks and obliterated opposing linemen. He would be a major star somewhere in college and it would be as a lineman, not a running back. They just needed about three or four more Dexters. But they would have to make do with the one they had.

Practice ended and Coach had still not heard from the Davis boys. He thought maybe that was a good thing. If the answer was "no," why would it take this long? He'd given the family a day or so to decide. And so far it was only one morning.

The opening regular season game was less than two weeks away, but Coach had arranged for a "controlled scrimmage" with nearby Harborside High School in less than a week. That scrimmage could give them some idea as to where this team is. Harborside was a private school, slightly larger than Coral, but nearly all boys. They had a reputation for having pretty good football teams. It would be a good test. At least hopefully. And the results would not count. That was probably a very good thing.

After the coaches had finished their after-practice meetings, Coach headed for his car. A small silver compact car pulled up. Coach glanced inside, hoping it might be the Davis boys. Instead, it was a young lady, short, smallish, kind of cute with short, light brown hair. She rolled down the window.

"You must be Coach Gayton." she said. "Is Dexter finished with practice?"

"And you would be?" queried the coach.

"Melinda," she said smiling. "Melinda Miller. I'm kind of Dexter's girl friend."

"He should be out any time now. In fact, here he comes."

"Nice meeting you, Coach!" said Melinda as Dexter came out and stuffed his big body into the passenger seat of the little car.

"See you tomorrow, Coach," yelled Dexter out the window as the car took off.

Coach waved goodbye, went to his car, and headed home.

When he arrived home it occurred to him that maybe he should get to know his players a little better. While coaching in college he had always made it a point to get to know all his players. Here, the team had been practicing for over two weeks already and he knew almost nothing about his players. Not that he would be prying into their private lives. Just a little about their families, their interests, their hobbies and such. Then he could at least converse with them about something other than football. Coach decided to start with Dexter.

Arriving home he again found the big house empty. It was still a bit early for lunch, so he wandered into the den, turned on his computer, and clicked on Google. Winston, the family cat, jumped on his lap as soon as he sat down. Winston, so named because Mrs. Gayton thought his face looked a bit like Winston Churchill, loved to sit in Coach's lap while he was typing away on the keyboard. But he also had the bad habit, at least Coach Gayton considered it a bad habit, of occasionally reaching out a paw and hitting one or two of the keys, invariably messing up anything Coach was trying to type.

Coach put one hand on Winston's head. Partly to pet him and partly to keep him from being able to reach the keyboard. Winston purred loudly.

Coach soon found that Dexter was the only child of Dr. Brendon and Mrs. Betty Middleton, and that "Dr. Ben," as he was usually called, was the town's veterinarian. In addition to an office "downtown," as if there really was a downtown Coral, the Middletons had a small farm and a large house about a half mile from Coral. And Mrs. Middleton was an English teacher at the high school. Dexter's dad had played college football at a small Midwestern college, He had received some slight interest from a couple of pro football teams, but was more interested in animals and veterinary medicine. He had done quite well as the local vet and was quite active in the Coral Chamber of commerce.

Winston's purring changed abruptly to a more plaintive tone, probably signaling he was ready for lunch. Coach decided that he was ready also and went to see what might be in the refrigerator. And, at least for the moment, Coach had most of the information he wanted. He could get more from Paul Horn tomorrow.

Practice the next morning was NOT going well. The quarterback, Ken Turner, was complaining that his arm was getting sore from all the throwing practice. Every player was accumulating various bumps and bruises, even though there had, at least so far, been no serious injuries. It was impossible to have the first string offense practice against the first string defense since so many of the starters played both ways. And the extra linemen used for the practice team were getting really tired of being pushed all over the field by Dexter. Coach Gayton called a halt and had everyone "gather up." His "gather round" and "listen up" had somehow gotten shortened to "Gather up!"

"Guys, I know that, at this point, this is all hard and probably boring work. No fun, no glory, just hard repetitive work. But doing the same job, running the same plays over and over and over again, while no fun at all, is necessary. So, when we get to the actual games, you don't have to THINK about all your assignments for each play, but they just flow naturally. Practice may or may not make perfect but it just about always makes better. We have to keep working and keep practicing. The good news is that next week we have the scrimmage with Harborside. We'll be able to start hitting somebody on another team. So, if we can just hang in there for another week, we will start seeing the positive results of all this hard work. All right? Now let's get back to work. And continue getting better!"

As the team headed back to practice, some of the young men still seemed unsure. Coach walked over to Lindy Patterson.

"Lindy!" he began. "I especially wanted to tell you how much better you have gotten. I have been really encouraged with your progress! Nobody has made a bigger improvement than you. You really do have some talent there!"

Lindy looked surprised. Coach had been very pleased with the progress Lindy had made, but he also sensed that all the drudgery and "blood, sweat, and tears" was taking a toll on him. He needed encouragement.

Lindy looked surprised. "Thanks, Coach!" he said with a renewed energy in his steps.

As Coach turned away from Lindy, he noticed a car pull up to the curb near the practice field. Wayde Davis and his brother got out. Coach headed toward them, not sure what to expect. Would this be the good news he was hoping for? Or bad news? At least he would know, one way or the other. And soon!

They met about half-way to the car. Coach was trying to think of something clever to say. But before he could say anything, Elston, the younger brother, blurted out excitedly, "Mom says we can play! She's still really worried about us getting hurt but we can play!"

"She says it's OK as long as she doesn't have to watch," Wayde chipped in!" What do we have to do now?"

Coach wanted to hug them both. He shook hands instead. They went into his office. Coach fixed them up with all the necessary forms and sent them for physicals. "Tomorrow we'll get you started and have you meet the team."

He just might have his quarterback!

CHAPTER 5
THE RESTART

The laws of physics say for every action there is an equal and opposite reaction. Or something like that anyway. Coach Gayton hadn't studied much physics since he was in high school and that was quite a long time ago. But he had always remembered that principle. That reaction was going to come from Kenny Turner. And the rest of the players. And maybe even from some other unexpected places as well. He couldn't just *give* Wayde Davis the quarterback job. After all, Kenny Turner had done every single thing Coach had asked him to do. He had worked hard. Coach figured that with an open competition, it would soon be obvious to everyone that Wayde was the far better quarterback and gave the team a much better chance to win. So, Coach quickly huddled with his assistants and announced the whole new game plan.

Then it was time to talk to the entire team. "Gather up, guys." he began. First he introduced the two Davis boys to the rest of the team. Then he discussed the new offense, with two running backs instead of the single back sets they had been practicing. That would give them an extra blocker. Whoever won the upcoming competition would be the quarterback but whoever *didn't* win would be a running back and there would be option passes for whoever that turned out to be. The quarterback battle would be between Kenny and Wayde. And Elston would be trying out for wide receiver and also kicking and punting.

It was only a week and a half before the scrimmage with Harborside. And now they would be almost starting over. There was a major improvement in the passing game, possibly the receiving corps, and most likely, punting and place kicking as well. However, it takes time to learn all the plays, certainly more than a week and a half. They would have to do the best they could.

As Coach suspected, it didn't take long to see Wayde's passes, with nice tight spirals, were mostly right on target and sailed a good thirty or even forty yards. Kenny's were wobbly and anything beyond ten yards was way off-target.

After about half an hour, Kenny walked over to Coach and said, "not much of a competition, is it? What do I have to do to play running back?"

Coach could see he was pretty dejected. But he was really pleased that Kenny wasn't going to quit.

"Could you help Wayde with our terminology and explain the plays?" Coach asked. "He's got a lot to learn and only about ten days to do it"

"I'll give it my best shot." said Kenny, as he headed over to where Wayde was still throwing to several of the receivers.

"You will still be throwing some passes!" yelled Coach Gayton. "I'll guarantee it." Then Coach turned to find Elston and see how he was doing.

Elston was a natural wide receiver. Good height at about 6 feet one, really good speed, and great hands. He would have to learn the passing routes, and how to block as well as catch, but he would easily be their best receiver. And a more than adequate punter. He would need to get his punts off a bit quicker, especially with a fairly weak offensive line. But he was a great upgrade. Maybe they could even teach him to kick field goals. The soccer kickers might be adequate for extra points but were pretty much useless for anything longer.

After a couple of days things settled into routines again. Wayde was picking up the formations and plays, with major help from Kenny. Kenny even showed some talent at running back. Although most of the blocking assignments were completely new to him, he already knew where all the plays were designed to go. And he had decent speed and was quick to the hole, assuming there actually was a hole. However, when there was no clear path and the play broke down, That was where he needed improvement. And the option passes that were added showed some real promise. It turned out that Kenny actually threw better running than he did standing in the pocket. Not when running for his life, but running, especially to his right, since he was right handed. Things seemed to be falling into place. If they would only fall fast enough.

It turned out that Wayde could move very well when he had to. He could quickly decide when no receiver was open, fake a throw and put the ball under his arm and outrun just about everybody. So the coaches designed a couple of plays around that. Red Granger was developing into a dependable runner and a pretty good blocker. Of course all this was against their own second team. The Harborside scrimmage would give them a real measuring stick to see if this progress was real or just showed up against inferior competition.

Then there began a series of injuries. Minor to be sure, but injuries, never-the-less. First Red Granger suffered a bruised knee. It wasn't really a bad bruise, but it definitely slowed him down and limited his ability to make cuts, a necessity for any running back. So Coach had to run practices without him. Temporarily, at least until Red recovered, the offense went back to one-back sets with Kenny Turner the lone running back. Then Bailey Grant developed a sore shoulder. Since he was the long snapper, that was a serious problem. And that also meant he was unavailable at left end which was an even bigger problem. Coach brought in Anthony Sparks, a back-up lineman, to take Bailey's place; however, Anthony was smaller, slower, and worst of all weaker than Bailey. The only good thing about that was that Anthony turned out to be a pretty good long snapper, so that would give some needed depth at that position. Fortunately, the rest of the injuries were less serious and involved reserve players rather than starters. But practice without Red and Bailey was not the same.

One other thing that Coach Gayton thought he noticed that might be a problem. Although he had listed camaraderie as one of the benefits of playing football, Wayde and Elston were not being accepted as well as Coach had hoped. Wayde and Kenny seemed to be getting along well, in spite of the uncomfortable positions in which they each found themselves. Kenny was trying to help Wayde better learn the quarterback position--the very position Kenny had wanted dearly and worked at with every ounce of energy he could muster. And Wayde, in spite of superior skills, was still learning all the plays and the formations. Plus Wayde was rather quiet by nature. Barking out signals loud enough for all eleven guys to hear was hard for him. Coaches and Kenny frequently had to remind him to actually yell out the signals. But he was getting the hang of it. However, Elston seemed to be all by himself most of the time. Coach wasn't sure if that was intentional on Elston's part or if there was some other reason.

At Vermillion Coach always had a really diverse collection of players. Character, of course, made a difference. But ethnicity, religion, and those types of things were irrelevant. If you could play, you did. And all were treated the same. Coach wanted it the same here. Wayde and Elston were among the very few minority students at Coral High School. Coach hoped race would have nothing whatsoever to do with this. But he wasn't completely sure. So he set about to find out. And if anybody had the pulse of this team, it would be Dexter.

The next day turned out to be really hot. One of those late summer days where a heavy morning fog took a long time to burn off and walking out of an air conditioned building felt like you were walking into a wall of oppressive heat and humidity. To make matters even worse, the wind was so calm not a blade of grass seemed to be moving. Fortunately school hadn't started yet so practice would be in the morning and could be ended early before it got to be unbearable. Unfortunately, both Red Granger and Bailey Grant were still out with injuries and the scrimmage with Harborside was now only a few days away.

By eleven o'clock the coaches felt they had gotten about all the workouts, exercise, and light contact drills the team could handle for such a hot day. Tomorrow was supposed to be a very similar day but with a chance of late morning rain, and then the forecast was for cooler weather after that. That, if it actually happened, would be very helpful and welcome.

Coach dismissed the team but called Dexter aside before he headed for the showers. "Dexter," coach began, "I need your help."

"Sure, Coach," said Dexter, a little unsure about what he was going to be asked to do.

"I need to know how well Lindy, Wayde, and Elston are being accepted by the team." Coach continued. "I know they didn't start when everybody else did. But they are all working very hard to learn the playbook. I specifically recruited them to join the team, even though we were well into practice by then. They have a lot to contribute, even though their addition means some of the original guys now might not play as much as they otherwise would have. I want them to be accepted by all their teammates. I don't want any hard feelings. Right now, I'm not really sure that is the case. If there is anyone on this team that knows what is going on 'behind the scenes,' Dexter, it's you. Can you check this out for me and keep me informed?"

Dexter looked a little surprised and more than a little confused. And he didn't want to get anyone in trouble, either. Dexter was a fun-loving guy and this sounded altogether too serious. " I...I guess I can check around..."

"Just let me know if there seems to be a problem," said Coach, sensing Dexter's discomfort. "I am not asking you to spy on anybody or anything like that, Dexter. I just want to have everybody on the team working together and pulling for each other. I don't expect you to investigate anybody or anything like that. Just let me know if there is any real dissension."

"I guess I can do that, Coach!" said the somewhat relieved Dexter. "I'll get back to you!"

Dexter was almost always in a good mood. He especially liked twisting old adages until they made no sense at all. He would ask, "You know what they always say?" followed by "People who live in stone houses shouldn't throw glass windows." or "A rolling moth gathers no stones." Or "When playing solitaire three cheats is fair." Or "Don't cover a book by its judge."

One of his favorite words was "Enthusiwasm, which he defined as "Like if you are driving around and having a really good day and all of a sudden a police car pulls you over for speeding." In that instant, according to Dexter, enthusiasm becomes enthusiwasm. Everybody who knew Dexter called them "Dexterisms."

Dexter was now filled with "enthusiwasm."

The day of the Harborside scrimmage turned out to be an almost perfect evening for football. Getting everything and everybody aboard two busses took some time, and there was some confusion and some misplaced equipment to deal with, but finally they were on the road. It was only about a 45 minute ride to Harborside but, for many of the players, it was their very first team bus ride and they were a bit unsure about the whole event. Soon the busses pulled into the Harborside High School parking and the team disembarked. The Harborside coach greeted the team and informed them as to where the showers and the field were and then turned to Coach Gayton.

"Welcome to high school football, Coach!" Borderline Head Coach Sherman said. "I gotta ask you, what possessed you to come out of retirement to take this job...and for no pay? I'm really curious.".

Coach hadn't given much thought to the kind of reception he would get from other coaches. He had been too busy trying to put a team together to worry about that. But it isn't every day that a high school gets to play against and possibly beat a College Hall of Fame coach.

"I think I just missed interacting with young people," answered Coach Gayton after a short pause. "And when Coral needed a coach with only a few weeks before the season started, I wanted to step up and accept the challenge."

"Well I expect you will have plenty of challenges all right! See you on the field." Then Coach Sherman headed back to his team.

CHAPTER 6
SOME ANSWERS, MORE QUESTIONS

The scrimmage lasted only a little over an hour. Harborside had two almost completely separate teams, one for offense and one for defense. Almost every player on Coral played both offense and defense. That created some endurance problems for Coral. In the long run it would help the Lancers develop some extra stamina but right now it just wore them out. During the regular season only two Cross County Conference schools had enough players to have a separate offenses and defenses. They were Borderline, a Class 3 team and Coral's opening conference game, and Windham, by far the largest school in the conference. Windham always dominated the conference and was currently rated the number three team in the state in class 5 while all the rest of the conference schools were in class 2 or class 3.

Lindy Patterson, at least for most of the scrimmage, played well. He and Dexter continuously opened big holes in the Harborside defensive line for Kenny Turner and even Wayde Davis to run through. Coral was still missing both Red and Bailey, but expected them back for the Borderline game. Defensively the line was good, but not dominating like Coach had hoped. Nobody got pushed around, but nobody got near the quarterback either. Offenses were just basic plays and reasonably predictable. Harborside did resort to double teaming Dexter near the end of the scrimmage, but Dexter never seemed to tire at all and still was very effective. Wayde was able to complete some nice passes, mostly on short crossing patterns, and mostly to his brother.

After the scrimmage was finished Harborside Coach Sherman came over to the Coral coach. "Good scrimmage!" he said. "Hey, we knew all about the Middleton kid but where did you find that quarterback? We *didn't* know about him. He's got some talent and great composure."

"He just enrolled in our school a few weeks ago. His dad is the new Coral Postmaster. And we are really happy to have him and his brother on the team!" answered Coach Gayton. They are a little behind the rest of the team as far as knowing the plays, but they are fast learners."

"Well, you've got some real talent there from what I can see," said Coach Sherman. "Good luck for the regular season."

"Same to you!" Coach Gayton replied as he turned and headed for the big yellow Coral buses..

The ride back to Coral was somewhat subdued but still cautiously boisterous. For the most part they had played well. Much better than expected. Still, they did wear down near the end when Harborside scored two of their three touchdowns. And they still had problems with the kicking game, both kicking and receiving. Coach was thinking of having Elston Davis do the punting and maybe even the kickoffs but that, added to mastering the passing routes and formations, was a lot to learn in such a short time. Their first actual game would be played in just a week.

Soon they arrived back at Coral. Coach knew he had to talk to the whole group before they all left for home, some with and some without their parents. After the entire team was off the bus he spoke loudly,

"Gentlemen. gather round and listen up!"

"First of all I want to tell each and every one of you how proud I am of of you. There are still a lot of things we have to work on but you put together a great effort. Now it is time to get ready for a real game, that counts in the standings, against a conference team, Borderline High School. It won't be easy, but worthwhile things are rarely easy. Let's go home and come back tomorrow ready for some good practices."

Dexter reported back to Coach that he detected no disrespect on the team toward any of the three late additions. Everybody understood that they gave the team a much better chance to win and he saw no animosity at all. This was really good news to Coach Gayton.

Following that, the coaches had a brief meeting inside the school in the athletics department office.

"Well, what did you think of the scrimmage?" asked Coach Gayton. Paul Horn spoke first. "I was pretty impressed with Dexter's ability to fight through double teams, both on offense and defense. And Lindy held his own and helped shut down some of their plays. He's gotten almost as strong as Dexter. Hopefully that will translate to nobody triple teaming Dexter like they did last year. And Wayde showed glimpses of a strong and accurate arm, a nice tight spiral, and, above all, a composure under fire that I didn't really expect this early in his career. He's got real potential."

Thad Holloway chipped in. "The defense wasn't bad for early in the season. Most of Harborside's success came on quick, short passes and runs to the outside while keeping Lindy and Dexter to the inside. Our linebackers, in particular, need to flow to the football quicker. But you can't teach speed, as they always say."

"If they could read their keys quicker that would definitely help. But they should get better as they get more experience. This is a whole new system for all these guys and, as far as I can see, everybody is giving it their best shot," said Coach. "That is all we can ask."

Their first opponent, Borderline High School, was actually a Class three School in size and, like Harborside, would have two almost completely separate offensive and defensive teams. So stamina would definitely be a factor. "We will have to play our back-ups or we'll be totally out of gas in the second half." observed Coach Gayton. "All other teams on the schedule will be more equal in size and numbers. Except our last game against Windham." Windham is a Class 5 school and is currently ranked as the third best team in that class. Over the years they had been invited to join bigger more challenging athletic conferences, but declined. They really enjoyed being the big bullies in the Cross County Conference. They were undefeated in the regular season almost every year and actually won the state Class 5 championship twice. But there would be plenty of time to worry about Windham in a couple of months. Right now they had to get ready for Borderline. That would be tough enough.

CHAPTER 7
READY OR NOT

The week sped by quickly. It was decided to have Wayde do the punting and Elston do the kick offs. That could make a definite difference in field position, since Wayde could punt the ball 35 to 40 yards and Elston could do about the same with kick offs. That was at least twice as far as anybody else on the team could kick. The coaches would have liked to have Elston run back kick offs and punts, but he was already learning all the passing routes and adding runbacks to his responsibilities, at this point, seemed a bit too much. So long snapper Bailey Grant had been practicing that and would have the job for now. All the injured guys were finally ready to play.

Were they ready? Hopefully... but ready or not, Saturday evening arrived right on schedule. On the bus to Borderline, Dexter was his usual, jovial self and he kept those around him pretty loose. The guys who had played last year seemed ready to play. Surprisingly, it was the substitutes who looked to be on edge. The new additions, Lindy Patterson, Wayde Davis, and Elston, seemed pretty calm for their very first game ever.

It was a beautiful night for football. Temperature was in the mid- seventies with only a slight wind. Quickly, the calisthenics

were started and finished. Everything seemed to zip by in a hurry and soon it was time for the National Anthem. The Borderline Glee Club led the singing and did it very nicely. Borderline won the coin toss and deferred to the second half. Given a choice, Coach Gayton would have preferred to kick off and take his chances on defense so his players could loosen up a bit before going on offense. Now he had no choice.

Borderline kicked off down to the Coral five yard line. Bailey got underneath the ball but took his eyes off it to look at the onrushing Borderline players and fumbled the football. The ball bounced into the end zone and was recovered by Borderline for a touchdown. A quick point after kick and it was 7-0 favor of the Bobcats. Borderline kicked off a second time, again down to about the Borderline five yard line. This time Bailey misjudged it completely and again it bounced into the end zone and was recovered by the Bobcats. Extra point and, in less than 30 seconds, the score was 14-0 Borderline. Coach went over to Elston and asked him if he thought he could catch the kickoff. Obviously, Bailey Grant wasn't cut out for running back kickoffs. Elston said he would give it a shot. Coach told him to catch the ball and head for the sidelines and run out of bounds.

"Avoid the tackle!" said Coach. "We need you healthy."

Elston did better than that. He caught the ball cleanly, started to head for the sidelines but saw an opening and cut back toward the middle of the field as Coach closed his eyes...while Elston made it up to the 25 yard line before getting out of bounds as he was told. Coach opened his eyes and took a deep breath. Kick offs and punts were probably the most dangerous plays as far as injuries are concerned. Quarterback sacks were probably second on that list.

A couple of short pass completions and it was third down and two yards to go from the Coral 33 yard line. Paul Horn called for a Red Granger run right up the middle behind Lindy and Dexter blocking. Going through a big hole, Red plowed ahead for five yards and a first down. Maybe there was hope. Paul called the run/pass option but on a pitchout misdirection to Kenny Turner. Kenny had a wide-open receiver but threw a terribly wobbly pass that was intercepted and run back for another Bobcat touchdown. No more than five minutes into the game and Coral was down 21-0.

Getting ready for the third kickoff, Coach gathered the team for a quick huddle up. "OK guys, we're in a pretty deep hole. We can do this. Everybody just has to do their own job, just as we practiced. Paul, let's switch to our running game and give them a steady dose of Lindy and Dexter."

That was the game plan. And it worked. Sort of. Coral went on a long drive, got down to the Borderline fifteen yard line but the drive stalled there. Elston tried a 32 yard field goal but it bounced off the right upright, no good. But they had definitely moved the football, and had run enough time off the clock that the quarter soon ended.

The second quarter was pretty uneventful, although Borderline was able to move the football close enough to kick a field goal as the half ended. 24-0 Bobcats at the half. Coach guessed it could have been worse. The teams left the field for halftime as the Borderline band marched onto the field.

CHAPTER 8

THE STREAK

Dexter had mercilessly harassed the Bobcat's quarterback, and he and Lindy disrupted the running game as well. The game plan for the second half would be to rely on the running game and only occasionally throw the ball. For the fourth quarter they would go back to the passing game. Coach, analyzing the Borderline defense, expected them to double team Dexter and possibly double team both Dexter and Lindy. That would put a lot of pressure on the Coral secondary and especially the linebackers. Coral could bring the linebackers closer to the line of scrimmage, which might help somewhat, but, if Borderline went to their passing game Coral's secondary would probably break down. Coach hoped that, with a 24-0 lead, Borderline would mainly stick to the running game.

Quickly halftime was over and Coral was ready to kick off. Elston lofted a nice high kick down to the Borderline twenty yard line where the returner managed to catch the ball and get to about their 31 yard line. A couple of first downs and a tackle for loss by Dexter forced a punt on fourth down and six. Elston had to fair catch the punt at the Coral 12 yard line. The double teams didn't materialize, at least not yet. Kenny Turner and Red Granger took turns running the ball with Wayde throwing in an occasional quarterback keeper. It took a while, but Coral worked their way down the field to a first and goal just inside the Borderline ten yard line. On first down, a Kenny Turner run netted five yards. Second and a short five. Borderline pulled everybody in tight. Not exactly double-teaming Dexter and Lindy, but really bunching up everybody in the middle. The play call was a fake handoff up the middle with Wayde running left and throwing if anybody was open, or running, if necessary. The entire defense bit on the fake and Wayde easily outran the one defender who stayed on the left side. Touchdown Coral! The entire team ran into the end zone and high fived Wayde. You would almost think they had just won a bowl game. Coach smiled. The game wasn't over yet. The Bobcats still led comfortably 24 to 7 but the Lancers still had a chance. It wasn't out of reach...at least not yet.

After that, Borderline did double team both Dexter and Lindy, and that did change both offensive and defensive strategies. Every passing play still seemed to result in somebody chasing the quarterback, and running plays all had to go wide left or wide right with the middle totally clogged. Coral did get one drive going near the end of the quarter but only got a 35 yard field goal by Elston Davis. After three quarters of play the score was 24 - 10 favor of Borderline.

The fourth quarter found a very tired Coral team. With both Major College and professional football having separate teams for offense and defense, if the offense can at least run the ball effectively, they can both run time off the clock and give their defense a rest. When almost everybody plays both offense and defense, nobody gets any rest even if they can run time off the clock. Lindy was the first starter to get a rest. He was still getting into football shape. But there was a pretty large drop-off when the substitutes came in for Coral. The Bobcats were able to run wide sweeps against the subs. and gain large chunks of yardage. They worked the ball down to a first and goal at the Coral nine yard line. But on fourth down and goal to go from the Coral two yard line, Dexter blew up the play and sacked the quarterback for a ten yard loss. With subs still in the game, the offense couldn't move the ball and Elston punted to the Bobcat 48 yard line. While Coral was still cycling through the rest for starters, the Borderline offense went on a steady drive that ended with a three yard touchdown run. With the point after it was 31-10 and that just about ended any chance for Coral. With the starters all back in, Coral went on a drive of its own which culminated with a 25 yard touchdown pass from Wayde to his brother that made the score a more respectable 31-17. When Coral finally got the ball back there was only a minute and a half left in the game. Wayde completed several passes but most were of the relatively short variety and time ran out before they could even get into field goal territory.

"The streak continues." thought Coach Gayton.

CHAPTER 9
ROCK CREEK ROCKIES

Coach took his team to the Borderline side of the field to shake hands and say "good game!" He had talked to the team beforehand describing how to be a gracious loser and how to be a good winner. He said that, in his opinion, to be good at anything you need lots of practice. He never wanted to get enough practice losing to become good at it. Gracious, yes. Good, no way. After all the hand shakings and "Good games" Coach Gayton sought out the Borderline coaches and wished them well for the rest of the season. Then it was time to get back on the buses and head back to Coral.

The team was quiet on the bus ride home. The team had actually scored 17 points. More than in any game last year. But they still lost. Giving away three touchdowns was disastrous. Theoretically, they might have won 17-10 without those three touchdowns. But the game might have been coached totally differently by both teams were it not for those 21 points. And he didn't want to blame Bailey Grant for the two messed-up kick offs. They had practiced returning kick offs, but not with the whole defensive team running at you. "That was probably my fault," thought the coach. What exactly was he going to talk about at the mini-meeting after they got off the bus? Coach wasn't sure. He disliked not having something prepared but he would have to wing it. What a coach says at a time like this, after the low point of a loss, can make or break his acceptance by the team. Do this right and the team will follow you through hades. Do it wrong and you can lose the team's trust completely.

All too soon the bus was pulling into the Coral High School parking lot. After everybody had piled out of the two buses, Coach said, "Gather up, guys!"

"First let me acknowledge this: We lost the game. The streak continues. 46 games without a win. Our number one priority is to win that first game, break the streak, and then go on and keep winning. And tonight we didn't do it. But in spite of everything that went wrong, you still kept fighting. You never quit. And I am proud of you for that.

I have always felt that there are basically three kinds of football teams. The first are bad teams. Bad teams find a way to lose. Even when everything, all the breaks of the game go their way, they still find a way to lose. Then there are good teams. As long as things go their way, they will win. If things start going wrong, they lose. Finally, there are great teams. No matter if everything goes wrong, they still find a way to win. Right now, I would say we are a good team. We just played a school that is considerably larger than we are. And we stood toe-to-toe with them and after a very rough start, we held our own.""But based on what I've seen, I think we can become a great team. I believe we are not only going to win one game and break the streak...but we are going to win a number of games, hopefully enough to be in the end-of-season tournament. That is my goal, and hopefully your goal, too. We have a lot of work to do starting Monday. We play Rock Creek here at Coral. They finished second in conference last year and have most of those players back this year. So again, it won't be easy. Let's go home, get some rest, and come in Monday morning ready to work. Enjoy your Sunday!"

Coach knew this wasn't the most eloquent pep-talk he had ever given. But it was from the heart. He believed what he said and hoped they did too.

Practice was good. The coaches put in a few new passing plays and worked with Elston, getting him more comfortable with kick offs and place kicking as well as passing routes and Wayde with yelling out signals, throwing the ball to someone other than his brother, and punting. Everything was starting to look good.

Then, on Thursday, Lindy Patterson sprained his ankle and had to miss practice. He also missed practice on Friday. Without Lindy to complement Dexter, there would be nobody to discourage the Rockies from double or triple teaming Dexter. This was a major problem. Anybody they put in for Lindy would be totally inexperienced and badly underweight to play tackle. Red Granger had played only cornerback on defense up until now but volunteered to fill in for Lindy if Lindy couldn't play.

Saturday morning arrived and Lindy was feeling "a little better." He said he would try to go. The day was warm, but it was an evening game and the temperature had dropped into the sixties with a ten mile-an- hour wind. All the pageantry with the two bands and the cheerleaders finished. The pregame festivities ended and game time arrived. Elston proved to be very good at kickoffs and punt returns and there were no fumbles or miscues. But, although Lindy tried his best, it was obvious from the very first series that he was in major pain. Coach put Red Granger in for Lindy and soon Coach's worst fears were realized. Red had never before played on the defensive line before and, although he knew the plays, he couldn't block anybody at all. To be fair, Red's blocking assignment outweighed him by forty pounds. Soon the Rockies double teamed Dexter. Dexter could only handle one side of the line and the Rockies would run plays, mostly runs, to Red's side of the line. Even pulling the linebackers closer to the line didn't help much. Fortunately, the Rock Creek quarterback wasn't a very good passer because the Coral secondary was vulnerable.

Offensively, Coral was improving. With the Rockies' defensive linemen running over poor, outmatched Red Granger, the passing game had to be quick short slant passes, emphasis on the "quick." And the running game had to be almost entirely to Dexter's side of the line. All that considered and with a few quarterback runs mixed in, the halftime score was 21-14 favor of Rock Creek.

Coral still had a chance. Coral received the second half kickoff. Elston ran it back to the Coral 25 yard line. One of Coach's half time adjustments was to have Kenny Turner double team Red Granger's opponent in the line. Another was to constantly switch Dexter from one side of the line to the other. Coral would break the defensive huddle as late as possible so the Rockies wouldn't know which side Dexter was on until after the play was called. That worked for a while but then Rock Creek started calling audibles to change the play if Dexter changed sides. When Coral was on offense it still worked fairly well.

With a series of short passes and a few runs mixed in, Coral marched down the field. Eventually they faced a third down and goal from the three yard line. Coach sent in the play, a run up the middle by Kenny Turner behind a block by Dexter who would line up in the backfield. Kenny had the option to go wide if the middle was all clogged up, or even pass if that was all that was open. Dexter plowed through the line, leaving a big hole that Kenny could have walked through. Elston's extra point was good and the game was tied 21-21.

Rock Creek then got the ball and went on a long drive of their own. They ran all the remaining time off in the third quarter and finally settled for a field goal to take the lead 24-21. The final quarter found Coral driving again. When they got into the red zone, however, they got called for offensive holding and ended up with fourth down and 15 at the Rockies' 20 yard line. Elston kicked the field goal and they were tied again at 24 all.

Long, sustained drives run a lot of time off the clock and soon the Rockies had the ball first and goal from the Coral three yard line with 25 seconds left in the game. Dexter broke through the double team and hit the quarterback as he tried to hand off the football. The quarterback lost the ball, ran back and recovered it, but it was now second and goal from the 12 yard line. Rock Creek called time with three seconds to go in regulation time. On the field goal try, Dexter again broke through the double-team and got a finger on the ball but it went through the uprights as time expired. Final score: Rock Creek 27 Coral 24. The streak continues.

CHAPTER 10
THE WARLOCKS

On Monday evening Dexter was working hard on the family's "Ranch." The family called it the "Second Chance Ranch" as it said on the big sign at the entrance. It consisted of about fifteen acres of fenced-in land with a large, heated farm building, and there were all kinds of animals at the ranch, including dogs, cats, cows, a horse, a couple of llamas, pigs, several deer, a pair of rheas, and various other animals that had been "given" to his dad, the local veterinarian. They all had to be fed, and that was one of Dexter's jobs. Besides, lifting and throwing hay bales around was building up his strength, and he liked that a lot more than lifting weights. He would still lift weights with his teammates, but that was more to get everybody on the team, or at least those that weren't farmers, to build up their strength with the weights. Besides, he knew when he went to college to play major college football he'd have to do it anyway, so this gave him a head start.

A big SUV pulled into the driveway, so Dexter went out to meet it. He wasn't expecting any visitors. The passengers started to get out of the car and the driver looked familiar. It was Anthony Thuley. Dexter and Anthony had met at last year's game between their two schools and had become friends. A large brown dog wandered over toward the car and the five passengers jumped back inside. Both Anthony and Dexter started laughing.

"He won't hurt you." said Dexter. "Just don't make any quick moves and you'll be fine."

"What brings you out here?" Dexter asked Anthony. "Did you come to concede Saturday's game to us?"

"No, not quite!" declared Anthony with a grin. Anthony had become something of a local rap star with a number of fairly successful albums.

Just then, a big black cat walked out of the barn toward the car. Dexter asked the cat "Ali, what kind of cat are you?" The cat stood up on his back legs and punched the air several times. "He thinks he's a boxer!" said Dexter and everybody laughed.

Anthony said "Hey, I might be able to put together a rap song about Ali, the boxer cat! And put it on my next album."

"Don't do that," said Dexter. He's already spoiled enough. And then I'd have to get him an agent!" And everybody laughed again.

"Seriously," said Anthony. "The reason we drove up here was that last year you offered to take us on a hay ride and we couldn't make it on that day. Is the offer still open?"

"Sure! The only thing is that it would have to be after the game. I think they have rules against fraternizing with other teams ahead of games. Something to do with gambling I believe. But any time after the game should be ok. I'll check with our coach. When did you want to come out?"

They settled on a date a few days after the game. Dexter asked if maybe hot dogs and chips would be ok for a snack and if he could invite the Coral team as well. "I know not everybody can make it, but we can invite them all anyway. A hayride around the property and seeing all the animals would take maybe 45 minutes or so, and we might have to make two or three trips."

"That would be great!" said Anthony. "I know a lot of our guys have never even seen a llama or a rhea. It should be fun. Did you know that we started a gardening project this year? We got the whole team involved. We planted all kinds of vegetables and herbs and stuff. When it is all finished, we will donate all the food to the needy families in the area. We even got some good press in the paper and that brought in more helpers. It turned into a really good project."

"Congratulations! Sounds great!" said Dexter. "By the way, we are having the first annual TRACI Movement parade in a couple of weeks. would you like to join us? It will be about a half mile of walking with free TRACI tee shirts. It will be here in Coral and you would be welcome to join us. It won't be huge, just a few floats and several high school bands and a lot of marchers and signs. Your band will be one of the bands. It's small but it's a start."

"Remind me after the game and I'll talk to our coach and the team," said Anthony.

"Oh, yeah, the game! I almost forgot about the game," said Dexter. "See you there!"

Anthony turned the car around and headed down the driveway to the main road.

Dexter went back to work feeding all the hungry animals. When he had finished, he called Melinda to see if she would be available to drive the new tractor to pull the second hay wagon. She said that shouldn't be a problem, as long as she didn't have to drive Lurch, the older tractor which was balky and prone to frequent breakdowns. Dexter said he understood. Lurch had just come back from the repair shop and seemed to be running well.

Saturday dawned as a clear, cool morning which gave way to a rather warm, early afternoon. Practice went well, as Lindy watched somewhat dejectedly from the bench. His ankle was coming along, but Coach felt it would be better if he had one more week of healing and rest. The team did look ready. They were gaining confidence every week and tried to remain upbeat in spite of the fact that they had now lost 47 games in a row.

After everybody had loosened up, warmed up, and the footballs stopped flying through the air, they got ready for the National

Anthem. The Coral and Salem high school choirs joined together and did a wonderful job singing. Then the coin toss which turned out to be heads when Dexter, the Coral captain, called tails. Coach wanted Dexter to always call tails, figuring that way should result in winning the coin toss just about half the time. Salem elected to receive. Coach would have chosen to kick anyway, so that was all good.

However, while the kickoff was both high and deep, the kick returner, Anthony Thuley, took it at the Salem five yard line and flat outran everybody to the end zone. Salem quickly was up by a 7-0 score. This was altogether reminiscent of the first game. However, Wayde connected on a couple of medium deep passes, then ran some time off the clock before he found his brother in the end zone for six points, and, with the point after, they were tied 7-7. They did it by staying away from wherever Anthony was on the field. He was obviously faster than anybody else on either team. And that was going to be a major problem all afternoon. Coral's fastest player was now Elston Davis with Roger Morrison a fairly close second. So Coach moved Elston to safety, alongside Roger.

The Salem quarterback was a better runner than passer. But with Dexter breaking through most double teams and with the Lancers' linebackers playing close to the line of scrimmage, Coral stifled most of the Warlock's running game. But with Anthony Thuley shadowing Elston on every play, the Coral offense didn't have much success either.

Late in the first half the score was still 7-7 with Salem having a third and eight from their own 23 yard line, Elston intercepted a short pass and ran it back to the end zone for a touchdown to put Coral up 14-7 as the half ended. For the first time ever in history, Coral actually had a halftime lead.

Halftime is a time of adjustments. Coach figured that if Anthony was going to take away Coral's only deep threat, the underneath routes would be open to short crossing patterns. If Elston could go deep and take Anthony with him, the rest of the Salem secondary didn't look all that effective. Most of Coral's yardage in the first half had come from Wayde's running...some of it designed but most of it from necessity. Kenny Turner and Red Granger could take turns running the slants and separating from Elston and the tight coverage from Anthony. The short passing game, coupled with occasional runs, would also take time off the clock.

Coral received the kick and Elston had a nice runback to his own 28 yard line. With a two back set, Coral put Red in motion to his left and handed the ball to Kenny Turner for a run behind Dexter. The run gained eight yards to the Coral 36. With a second down and two, it was time to try the longer pass. The play worked to perfection. Elston came out of the crossing route and went deep down the right side of the field, taking Anthony with him. Red Granger caught the pass about 10 yards downfield and headed down the left side of the field. Red was able to get all the way down to the Salem five yard line before Anthony, who had to go all the way across the field after chasing Elston, caught up with him and brought him down. Two running plays behind Dexter blocks took it inside the one yard line. One more run and Coral, with the PAT, had a two-touchdown lead. Everybody was ecstatic! From the players to all the Coral fans, everybody was celebrating. As CoachGayton sent the defense out onto the field after the kickoff, he reminded everybody that there was still almost a full half to be played. He didn't want them to get overconfident.

About midway through the third quarter, Salem used Anthony as a wide receiver on the right side of the formation, then put him in motion to the left side. The Warlock quarterback faked into the line and handed ball to Anthony as he sped by. Once again Anthony outran the entire Coral defense into the end zone. With the PAT, it was Coral still leading 21-14. Late in the quarter Coral completed another crossing pattern but the cornerback on that side stopped Red for a gain of about 12 yards to the Lancer 40 yard line. Three running plays led to a fourth down and two yards to go at their own 48.

Coach called a time out. This was a tough decision. If Coral doesn't make at least two yards, they give the ball to Salem around midfield. Salem would probably bring everybody up close to the line with just the safeties back. If Dexter could still block the two or three guys in front of him, they could make it. Then there was the confidence factor. Do you show your confidence in Dexter and the team by going for it? Coach elected to go for it. The offense headed back out to the field. Dexter was able to get a fair block, even though he was triple teamed. Red Granger tried to hit that hole but stumbled a bit. He made first down yardage but was hit hard and fumbled the ball backward. He was able to get the ball back, but recovered it just short of the first down.

From that spot right near midfield, the Warlocks were able to move the ball down to the Coral 23 yard line. Facing a fourth down and five, they kicked a field goal and the score was 21-17 as the quarter ended.

It was becoming obvious that the triple teams were having an effect on Dexter. He really needed a break, but he was the key to the entire offense and defense. The only rest he got was not playing on special teams. Coach reluctantly sent the offense out for the final quarter, minus Dexter. Coral received the kickoff and the sure-handed Elston brought the ball out to the 21 yard line. Coral tried a couple of running plays that netted two yards. Then a pass attempt that saw Wayde running for his life and losing five yards. The punt went about 35 yards and the runback brought the ball to the Coral 41. Salem, seeing Dexter's absence, ran the ball right up the middle for gains of five, then eight, then 12 yards. First and 10 at the Coral 16. Dexter came up next to Coach. It was a very short break, but Dexter said he was rested enough. Even a tired Dexter was their best chance. Coach reluctantly sent him back into the game.

The next Warlock play was supposed to be a run up the middle, but when the Salem coaches saw Dexter back in the game in the Coral line, they quickly called time out. They changed the play and called for Anthony to line up at wide receiver...the same play they scored on earlier. But the slightly rested Dexter broke through the line and drove the quarterback right into Anthony who dropped the ball. He recovered, but it was a loss of five yards. On second and fifteen they tried to run wide, but the Coral linebackers stopped the running back for only a two yard gain. They tried a passing play on third and 13, but Dexter again broke through and the quarterback threw the ball out of bounds. On fourth down and seven the Warlock place kicker lined up, successfully made the field goal, and the score moved to 21 - 20, still in favor of Coral.

After that, neither team could move the ball. After exchanging punts several times and with only 20 seconds left in regulation, Coral punted on fourth and six. Anthony was deep for Salem. It was a good punt, but it gave Anthony a head start before Coral could get to him. Anthony streaked down the sideline until he was pushed out of bounds by Roger Morrison and Elston Davis at about the Coral 12 yard line. Six seconds left in the game. The Warlock kicker lined up and kicked the ball right down the middle as time expired. Final score: Salem 23 Coral 21. The streak continued.

CHAPTER 11
THE HAY RIDE

Both the fans and the team were in absolute shock. Just when a win had finally seemed not only possible, but likely, in a few seconds it all fell apart. Stunned silence filled the stands, contrasted with the happy team from Salem.

The two teams lined up and shook hands. When Dexter and Anthony got together, they each hugged. "Boy, I'm glad we don't play you again," said Dexter. "You were responsible for about 20 of your teams 23 points. You were a one-man wrecking crew!"

"Yes and so were you," said Anthony. "We couldn't do anything up the middle. I am sure glad I didn't have to block you. By the way, what did you want to remind me about?"

"Oh yeah, you were going to make sure it was ok with your coach to march with us in the Traci Movement Parade next Saturday," Dexter remembered. "It starts promptly at 9:00 a.m. Right here at the football field."

"Coach said it's fine as long as we don't do anything to reflect badly on the team," Anthony answered. "You said something about a float. Maybe we could make a simple float showcasing our Community Garden project. Then, if you can loan us one of your hay wagons, we wouldn't have to walk so much. After all, both teams have to play games later that afternoon."

Dexter thought that would be a good idea for both teams...and they did have two hay wagons. "Then we'll see you Tuesday evening at the ranch?" asked Dexter.

"You bet!" said Anthony. "Looking forward to it!"

At about 6:00 Tuesday evening, Dexter had finished feeding all the animals when a delivery truck pulled into the Ranch and dropped off a load of hot dogs, buns, chips, condiments, ice, cups, plates, and assorted soft drinks. As the truck was leaving, cars full of happy and excited football players started pulling into the lot. Dexter put them to work moving all the "stuff" closer to the barn and out of the still fairly hot sun. Soon the lot was almost full. Dexter was a little afraid that the two teams would sit with their own teammates, but what happened was the exact opposite. The players sought out their opponents from the game and congratulated each other on the hard-fought contest. "Perfect!" thought Dexter.

Just then Melinda drove up. Dexter thought this would be a good time for introductions. So he introduced Melinda first, then all the Coral players by position. Then it was Anthony's turn and he did the same, although kind of rap style. There were only a few missing from each team with guys having prior commitments. So, there would be at least two fully loaded hay wagons. Maybe even three. Dexter laid out some ground rules for the hayride such as "No jumping off while the hay wagon is moving "Because it's a long way down to the ground and we definitely don't want anybody getting hurt!" yelled Dexter for all to hear. Melinda started up the new tractor and headed around the perimeter of the Ranch. With a bit of adjusting, they got everybody on the two wagons.

Dexter fired up the second tractor. Over the loud noise of the big diesel he shouted, "Gentlemen, this is Lurch! He's called 'Lurch' because he occasionally lurches. Lurch is fifty-some years old so he's not just older than each of us, he's probably older than our parents. Just so you know that, if there are a few lurches here and there, you understand." Then Dexter put Lurch in gear and headed off to follow Melinda and the new tractor.

The items of interest started with an old-fashioned windmill, which pumped water into a large tub for all the animals. Then a big new windmill that provided some of the electricity for the Ranch. Further along was a small field of solar cells, which provided more electricity. Then there was a fairly large pavillion/shelter for picnics. Dexter thought it would be better to have the refreshments back near the barn because, for one, it was a long trip to the shelter, and two, they could sit on the hay bales and get more bales if they were needed since they were kept in the barn. Earlier Dexter had moved all the pavilion grills back near the barn and loaded them up with charcoal. The Ranch was a well-maintained scenic area and Dexter's dad sometimes rented out the shelter for picnics and had even had a wedding or two on the property. There was also a small kiddy playground with a rideable llama and other fiberglass animals custom designed to match the real ones. At the far end of the property was a utility pole with bright lights to go with the lights in the shelter. And atop the same pole was a tornado warning siren hooked into the town's system.

Everyone who hadn't been there before was duly impressed. "Wow!" said Anthony. "This is quite a place!"

They headed back to the big barn. Dexter got all the grills lighted and he and Melinda passed out all the dishes, hot dogs, chips, condiments, and drinks. It took some time to get all the hot dogs cooked, but everybody was having too good of a time to even notice. By the time everyone was done eating, it was sunset. It was a most beautiful sunset at that. Then they all milled around, petting the animals until it was almost completely dark. Nobody seemed ready to have it end.

Dexter met up with Anthony. "Hey, Anthony, I got a quick question. I looked up your latest rap album online the other day. Why in the world would you call yourself 'Anathema Thudley?' I like the Thudley part, but you don't want to be an anathema! That is like an outcast. It has a really bad connotation."

"Well," said Anthony, "I was going to look up the definition but I never actually got around to it. I just thought it was a really bad dude. And Anathema Thudley sounded close to Anthony Thuley, only better."

"First of all," said Dexter, "there's nothing wrong with your real name. But if you need a special rap name, how about just 'Thudley'? That's like the sound you make when you bring the receiver to the ground."

"Let me give that some thought!" replied Anthony. "And thanks so much for the hay rides and snacks. Most of our guys had never even seen a tractor or a hay wagon, let alone ridden on one. And petting the animals was fun. Even seeing Ali the boxer cat again cracked everybody up. We really appreciate this. Maybe we can reciprocate sometime...especially if you like barbecued ribs."

"That would be great!" responded Dexter as they shook hands, then gave each other a big hug. "Thanks for bringing everybody!" said Dexter. "Otherwise we would have been stuck with a whole load of food! See you Saturday morning?"

"You bet!" exclaimed Anthony' waving as he was leaving.

Finally it was just Dexter and Melinda. "Thanks for all your help!" said Dexter. "I couldn't have done this without you."

"Oh, I am sure you would have found a way." said Melinda.

"Even if that were true, it wouldn't have been as much fun. You do so much around here...you make everything work, especially when Dad or I are gone." said Dexter.

"Your Dad pays me quite well! And I'm glad to help." responded Melinda. After the two of them had gathered up all the leftover stuff and garbage and bagged everything for the next mornings' trash pickup, Melinda was about to leave.

Dexter leaned into her car and gave her a kiss. "See you tomorrow after practice? asked Dexter.

"Sure!" she answered. "You bet!"

When Dexter arrived home the first thing his dad asked was, "How did your hay ride go?"

"Couldn't have been better, absolutely couldn't have been any better!" Dexter answered.

THE ONLY THING WE HAVE TO HATE IS HATE ITSELF!

CHAPTER 12

THE PARADE

S aturday came quickly. Dexter had to feed the animals and get all his chores done early, then pull the now decorated hay wagon from the Ranch to the football field where the team would put the finishing touches on it. Then he had to make sure the Salem team, which had borrowed the Ranch's second hay wagon, had it lined up for the parade on time. Fortunately, there was no real wind to contend with, so they didn't have to worry about things blowing off the floats. That helped a lot.

It turned out there were four separate bands: Coral High School Band, Coral 8th grade band, Coral 7th grade band and Salem High School band. There were Coral's cheerleaders, Coral's 8th grade cheerleaders, and Salem's Cheerleaders. And three floats: the Ranch float withmuch of the Coral football team riding on it, pulled by Dexter, the Salem float, which many of the Salem team would ride on, pulled by someone from Salem in a pick-up truck, and a City of Coral float, which was professionally designed and appeared in almost every parade in this part of the state. The Salem float did have a miniature garden with a sign saying "Salem Community Gardens," as well as numerous signs about the Traci Movement.

One banner said "I Hate Hate " Another read "Love your neighbor as yourself"

And there were many others.

The TRACI Movement was an interracial movement started by Dexter, supported by his family and several local people of all races. It basically said "Talk is Cheap" and "Let's Actually Do Something." TRACI stands for "Try Respect And Compassion Instead," meaning instead of all the political correctness which seems to say if you change a few words around everything will be ok. These concepts were reflected in all the signs, posters, and decorations.

The city of Coral also provided several fire engines, and an old car club brought a number of antique cars. It was going to be a rather short parade, but as Dexter said, it was a start.

The whole ensemble worked its way slowly through downtown Coral. The bands each stopped to play a song so that added to the time length of the parade. Still, only about half an hour later and the TRACI parade was over. Dexter got good feedback from everybody involved.

"It was short but it was good and it was fun!" said one of the band members.

"I hope you do it again next year! Coral doesn't have very many parades." said another.

"I really like the theme." said another. "If we can all respect each other maybe we can put an end to all of the hate!"

"That was the whole reason for the parade." answered Dexter, pointing to one of the signs on the Coral float that said in big letters "The Only Thing We Have to Hate is Hate Itself."

Dexter wound his way through the small crowd milling around the three floats to find Anthony and the driver of the pickup truck pulling the second hay wagon. He could follow Dexter back to the Ranch. "Well, what did you think of the parade?" he asked Anthony. "I know it was short."

"Hey. It was short but it was really good! said" Anthony. "Maybe we can borrow some of your signs. I really liked that 'Hate' sign."

"Our small weekly newspaper was here and got some good pictures and I know they had nothing but positive things to say about the whole thing," said Dexter. "Actually, there were several newspapers here. I really appreciate you guys coming out to join us. It means a lot to me. Listen Anthony. Keep in touch. I'd really like you to join with us with our little movement!"

"Will do! It was fun!" said Anthony.

Then a newspaper reporter cornered Dexter for an interview. "Well, this is our kickoff project. We want everyone to 'Try Respect And Compassion Instead' of all the nonsense about changing a few words around and calling it political correctness and thinking that will really make any difference. We want action and we want mutual respect and we want compassion, not just talk." said Dexter.

The people had mostly left and Dexter talked to the Salem pickup driver so the two of them left the football field and headed back to the Ranch, each pulling a hay wagon. After all, each team did have a game that evening.

CHAPTER 13
WITHOUT A DOUBT

The Shady Elm Owls were next on the schedule for Coral, and it was an away game. Coach could tell that his team was pretty devastated by the last-second loss to Salem. However, after the hay ride and the camaraderie that developed between the two teams and how much respect the teams had for each other, Coral was not feeling particularly depressed. Coach's after-game speech concentrated on the positives, and he now felt the team would really rally together.

Shady Elm could be tough. They were more of a passing team so Coral would have to make some adjustments, but the Owls did NOT have any Anthony Thuleys which should make this game a bit easier. The offensive game plan would basically be the same with some tweaks. Lindy's ankle was healed now so that was a major difference. Red would not have to play tackle. But coach liked having Elston at safety, and the younger Davis seemed comfortable at that position where he could best utilize his speed.

It had been a busy week, especially for Dexter; first the hay rides and all that had entailed, then the parade, and now the football game. Hectic, busy, and time consuming, but extremely rewarding. Now if they could just get a win and break "the streak" it would all be good.

The bus ride was about half an hour long. It wasn't really quiet but everything seemed more businesslike with players comparing notes on techniques and such. They had talked to the Salem team at the hay ride and had a better idea of what they were doing that worked and what hadn't. And now they had Lindy back and that, they knew, would help a lot and lighten Dexter's workload a great deal. As they filed off the busses, they seemed to have a quiet confidence.

It was another nice evening for football, with mild temperatures and virtually no wind. The bands enthusiastically played and marched off the field. Once again, Dexter called tails for the coin toss. This time it came up tails. Playing a hunch, Coach had told Dexter that, if he won, to elect to receive.

The Owl's kickoff was nice and long and deep, but Elston managed to get the ball up to the Coral 30 yard line. The first play called was a misdirection run, sending Red in motion to the right side, faking the handoff to him, then handing the ball to Kenny going to the left side. Wayde pulled off the perfect fake. The entire defense followed Red into the right side of the Coral line while Kenny took the ball 70 yards down the left side for a touchdown. With the point after it was a quick 7-0 but this time in favor of Coral. Coach thought maybe it was a good omen

Shady Elm got the ball but couldn't contain either Lindy or Dexter and quickly faced a third down and 14. They attempted a pass but, with both Dexter and Lindy bowling their way through the Owl's line, the quarterback had to run for his life and was tackled back at his own 10 yard line. The punter had to hurry his kick and Elston took the ball at the Shady Elm 35 and hustled his way down to the 20 yard line. Two passes and a Wayde Davis run and Coral was up 14 to nothing. Less than five minutes into the game and total domination by Coral. "There's still a lot of time left!" Coach reminded the team as he sent the players out to kick off again. The rest of the quarter went about the same. On offense Dexter and Lindy kept opening big holes right up the middle and

Kenny, Red, and Wayde ran through the Shady Elm defense like they weren't there. On defense, at worst Dexter and Lindy totally blocked up the middle of the line and forced every run out wide where the linebackers were waiting. And, on every pass attempt, the Owl quarterback was getting harassed by Dexter or Lindy, or both. As the first quarter ended, Coral had another touchdown and a field goal for a 24-0 lead. Even the field goal could have probably been a touchdown. On a fourth down and two from the Shady Elm fourteen yard line, if the game had been closer Coach would have gone for the first down.

In the second quarter Coach put in a few substitutes. But a 24 point lead is not insurmountable. Concerned that Lindy might reinjure his ankle, Coach put Red in to replace him on defense but returned all other starters.

Dexter still dominated the middle of the line for the Coral defense and for the rest of the first half, the Owl's offense never got past midfield. The Lancer offense wasn't quite as effective and, for the most part, stayed with the ground game. They still scored two more touchdowns before the half ended with a lopsided 38-0 lead. In the locker room at halftime Coach was ecstatic.

"The streak is over!" He shouted. "Great job guys! Fantastic! Now we can forget about it and just play football. The only adjustments will be that our subs will play the second half. Kenny will be the quarterback. We will stick with the ground game almost completely. Here's your chance to play guys! Show us what you can do!" And he sent them out to the field.

Somewhat surprisingly, the Shady Elm coach also sent out his so-called "second string." The Coral substitutes surprised Coach Gayton and probably themselves and everybody else, by scoring a touchdown and two field goals while holding the Owls to just one field goal. When the clock showed the end of the game, the score read Coral 51 Shady Elm 3. Coral had ended "the streak" convincingly! "Without a doubt!" thought Coach Gayton. "Without a doubt!"

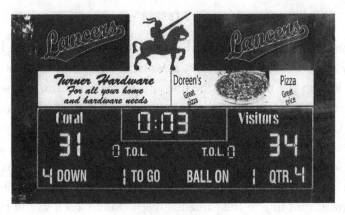

CHAPTER 14

HOMECOMING PART 1

Next on the schedule were the Clifford Lake Hawks, and they were undefeated so far with a 4-0 record. They would be a much tougher test than Shady Elm had been. But Coral was in a jubilant mood on the bus ride back to Coral. Coach was lavish in his praise of everybody. Even the subs had done well, and that was what Coach had feared was the weakest part of the team.

As they left the bus, Coach reminded them that this was Homecoming week and that there would be Coral alumni at the game that had never seen a Coral victory. "Can we show them how it's done?" asked Coach.

"You bet!" answered the team with loud and jubilant voices. "We'll be ready!"

Monday's after-school practice went really well, but for some reason Dexter didn't seem to be his usual self. He did everything he was supposed to do, but he was normally cracking jokes and such but today he seemed very serious. Very un-Dexter-like. After practice Coach thought he might ask Dexter if anything was wrong but, before he had a chance, Dexter came to him. "Can I talk to you for a minute?" asked Dexter.

"Sure Dexter, you can talk to me anytime." said Coach. "What is the problem?"

Dexter hesitated, but he valued Coach's opinion and wanted his input. "Well, as you know, Saturday night is the Homecoming dance. Everybody tells me I will be elected Homecoming King and Jessica Janes will be elected Queen. Jessica is one of the cheerleaders and she's very pretty and she's asked me to the dance. I know the king and queen are supposed to start off the dance but Melinda and I grew up as neighbors. We've known each other since before we could even walk. I do not want to hurt her feelings and I care a lot about her. But I don't want to hurt Jessica either. Any suggestions?"

Coach didn't know Melinda very well and he didn't know Jessica at all. "From what you just explained," he said thoughtfully, "I would simply tell Jessica what you told me. She must already know that Melinda is your girlfriend. Then ask Melinda to the dance. The sooner Jessica knows you can't accept her invitation, the sooner she can find another date. Does that make sense to you?" Coach asked. "My wife and I have been married for 40 years, so I don't really have any recent experience. But that is what I would do."

"Thanks, Coach, I really appreciate it." said Dexter. "See you tomorrow."

Coach had never before seen the serious side of Dexter. He hoped Dexter would get everything resolved before the game. A distracted Dexter was the last thing either he or Dexter needed.

A little later, Melinda picked Dexter up to drive him back to the Ranch. "Would you go to the Homecoming Dance with me?" Dexter blurted out.

Melinda was a bit surprised. "I thought you were going with Jessica." she said.

"She asked me but I told her no. I want to go with you. Of course I want to go with you. You're my girlfriend!"

"I don't have a dress. I wasn't planning to go. Did you and Jessica break up already?"

Dexter paused. "We were never together to break up. Right

before practice she asked me and I said no." Dexter might have fudged the timeline a bit but this was all basically true. "I'll go with you and we can pick out a nice dress tomorrow after practice." said Dexter.

"Are you sure that is what you want?" Melinda asked. "Jessica is a beautiful girl and I'm REALLY just the girl next door. I think you are just trying to spare my feelings. But I will survive!"

"But I won't," said Dexter. "And I think you are beautiful!"

The car drove up the driveway to the Ranch. Dexter asked her if she could stay for a little while and just talk. She finally agreed. Dexter could tell she was still a little hurt by the whole scenario. Dexter spoke first.

"In a few months I will be leaving Mom and Dad's house and the animals and the business and the Ranch. I have been offered a full ride scholarship to Vermillion University. Coach talked to the people there and got it all arranged. And they have one of the best veterinary programs in the country. Plan A was, if you were going to stay at your dad's place, you could take care of the Ranch and even continue helping my dad as an assistant. More pay of course. Now I have a brand new Plan B, assuming you are interested."

"Well, I certainly want to hear it first!" Melinda said, at least a bit skeptical.

"Hang on and here goes." Dexter began. "First of all, I'd like to get married. I know we haven't talked about it and this is a bit of a shock.

And, it may sound altogether too much like a business deal but I love you and can't imagine life without you. We have been together since we were both in strollers. I've always liked you, but somewhere along the line it became much more. I really want to marry you. You can pick the time and place and the kind of wedding but, after we graduate, I would like to get married. My mom and dad put aside a great deal of money for my education, but only if I went to school to become a vet. With my scholarship, I don't need the money. There is enough money to cover up to eight full years including vet school.

With the new name, image, and likeness rules, there should be at least a fair amount more. I talked to my mom and dad and, if we get married, it will all be yours. Dad wants to retire when we are all done with school and he will turn the business over to us. You and I would be full partners. I think your dad might be interested in taking care of the Ranch while we are away at school. Dad will pay him well. Dad will also pay for the wedding, as long as it doesn't get too expensive, and he wants to buy 2 or 3 acres of your dad's land adjacent to the Ranch and will pay above the going rate for farm acreage. If they move to Florida or someplace warm upon retirement, we would inherit their house. If not, they will help us build a new one on the 2 or 3 acres. OK, that is Plan B. What do you think?"

Melinda was stunned. "You'd actually do all this? I certainly care about you, too. You know I love animals and I had thought about trying to become a vet assistant or whatever they call it. But I never even dreamed..."

"How about I give you some time to think about it?" asked Dexter. "Now, one more time, will you go to the dance with me?"

"Of course I will! Of course!"

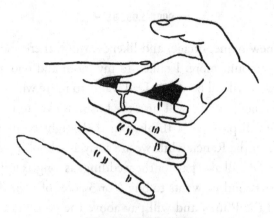

CHAPTER 15

HOMECOMING PART 2

Since the losing streak was now a forgotten thing, hopefully not to be ever brought up again, Coach wondered if the stands would be anywhere near full. The Salem game had been the first home game of the year, and the bleachers were about two thirds full for that game. The contest was so close that everybody pretty much stayed to "the bitter end." This game being Homecoming maybe, just maybe, the stands would be full. The game had been moved up an hour to five o'clock to allow more time for the dance. At 3:30 pm when the gates opened, there was already a line to get in. That was a good sign.

All the pregame festivities were done and everybody was anxiously awaiting the singing of the national anthem. It had become a tradition that the two school choirs or the two bands would perform the anthem but, since Clifford Lake had brought both their choir and band, all four, the two bands and the two choirs, performed together. The combined effort drew a good round of applause. Dexter once again called tails, but this time the coin toss came up heads. And Clifford Lakes chose to receive. It had been a sunny day with little wind and temperatures in the middle 60's. Almost another perfect evening for football.

Elston kicked the ball fairly high and deep, and the Hawks receiver made it back to his own 24 yard line. On first down the Clifford Lakes game plan became evident. The formation spread the offense over the entire field, put a man in motion to the right side and handed off to that running back for an eight yard gain before the linebackers could catch up to him. A cheer went up from the Hawks section of the stands. Obviously a fair sized contingent of their fans had made the twenty mile trip to Coral for what they expected would be an easy win for their undefeated team. But the stands were nearly full, and the great majority were pulling for the Lancers. On second and two, a fake handoff into the line ended up with a quarterback keeper around left end netted about five yards and a first down. The Hawks mixed in a few short, quick slant passes but stuck mainly with runs to the outside.

The Lancers dug in and finally stopped the drive, setting up a fourth down and four at the Coral 18 yard line. The Hawks managed to kick the field goal to open the scoring. 3-0, favor of Clifford Lake.

Coral took the kickoff and marched down the field to the Hawk's 21. Facing a fourth down and six, Coach decided to go for it. Wayde found his brother all alone in the end zone and lofted a perfect pass to him. With the PAT, it was now Coral 7 Clifford Lakes 3. A lot more cheers now, and a lot louder. The Hawks strategy was to make Dexter and Lindy constantly run from side to side and wear them out. Coach was again trying to compensate by bringing up the linebackers. Now he added bringing up the cornerbacks, too. That left only the two safeties deep. Sometimes that worked and sometimes it didn't. When it didn't work, it left Elston running down the pass receivers after long gains. For the remainder of the half, Clifford Lake scored two touchdowns and Coral had a touchdown and a field goal. The halftime score was 17 all. Coach could easily see that the Hawks' strategy was working. Both Lindy and Dexter were running wide on almost every play, plus both were getting doubled on almost every play. Coach had pulled each of them out for a few plays, but the Hawks took quick advantage and that resulted in one of their two touchdowns. Coach told the two of them that if on any play they pretty much knew they couldn't make the tackle or disrupt the play, they shouldn't waste much time chasing whoever had the ball. "I need both of you fresh and rested as much as possible for the fourth quarter!" asserted Coach.

While Dexter and Lindy still made a few defensive plays and kept the Hawks from any success with plays up the middle, the Hawks' passing game netted two touchdowns. With the two big linemen still opening gaping holes on offense, Coral scored one touchdown and was driving toward another as the third quarter ended. 31-24 in favor of Clifford Lake.

Using the running game runs time off the clock and, as Wayde connected with another nice pass to Kenny for the tying score, there were only about three minutes left in regulation. The Hawks got the ball and ran it back to their own 30 yard line. Their quarterback connected on another quick slant route, and suddenly they were in field goal range at the Coral fifteen yard line. Dexter put on a burst of speed and, caught the quarterback on a designed run, and pushed him out of bounds for a ten yard loss. On second and third downs, passes fell incomplete. On fourth and 20 from the Lancer 25, Clifford Lake kicked the field goal to take a 34-31 lead with two minutes left.

With a series of short sideline passes Wayde moved the team steadily down the field. It became fourth down and goal from the three yard line and only three seconds left in regulation. Tension was high on both sides, but especially so with Coral. After all, they had already lost multiple games right at the end. They could probably kick the easy field goal and send the game into overtime. Or they could go for it. Coach Gayton decided on the latter. The play call was a fake handoff up the middle with Wayde keeping the ball and running it in on whichever side seemed most promising or passing it if anyone was open. As they lined up, the Clifford Lake coach called time out.

As the team huddled again, Dexter addressed the group. "Well you know what they always say..." said Dexter.

"What's that?" responded Wayde as the whole team listened intently for some piece of wisdom from Dexter.

"The grass is always darkest on the other side of the silver lining!" said Dexter. Everybody stood silent for a few seconds, then they all burst out laughing. The tension was broken. The new problem they had now was they were all laughing so hard they would never get the play off in time. Wayde had to call another time out.

On the sideline again, Paul said, "Scratch that play. After seeing you guys laughing so hard the Hawks are going to expect some kind of trick play. Wayde, run right up the middle behind Lindy and Dexter."

Instead of jamming up the middle of the Coral line, the Hawks spread wide. Dexter and Lindy opened a hole up the middle that the Coral bus could have driven through, and Wayde walked into the end zone. Game over! Coral kicked the PAT. Lancers 38 Hawks 34.

"You sure know how to break the tension!" Coach said to Dexter over all the jubilant voices in the Coral locker room.

"I just thought maybe a little humor might help." said Dexter. "But I am sure glad we had that last timeout left!"

"Me too!" said Coach.

Dexter only had a little time after changing out of his uniform and showering to go home, get dressed and pick up Melinda for the dance. Melinda looked really good in the new dress she and Dexter had bought and Dexter told her so. "YOU are drop dead knockout gorgeous!" exclaimed Dexter.

They arrived at the dance. Everyone was buzzing about the game and especially the ending. At last Coral had won a close one. But Dexter had one more thing to do, and it was most important. And it could make or break his whole future, let alone the day.

The dance started with the formal announcement that the Homecoming King was Dexter Middleton and the Queen was Jessica Janes. The two of them started the first dance. After that, the second dance featured Jessica and her date and Dexter and Melinda. Then everyone else joined them. After several dances there was a short break. Dexter led Melinda out to the middle of the gym, got down on one knee and proposed. " Melinda Moore, will you marry me?"

There was a very short pause. What if she says" no" thought Dexter. He had only given her a few days to think about it. If she says "No" he would be totally humiliated, not to mention devastated, right in front of the whole school. The pause felt like an eternity but was in fact only a few seconds.

"Yes!" said Melinda. "Yes, I will marry you!"

Everybody cheered wildly as Dexter placed a diamond engagement ring on her finger.

"What a day!" said Dexter to Melinda.

Melinda said,"Tonight you were elected King. " That should make me at least a princess. Tonight I feel like a princess!"

"You <u>are</u> a princess!" said Dexter.

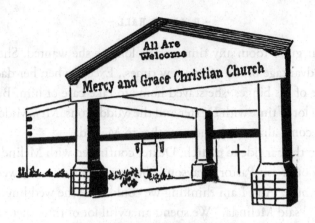

CHAPTER 16
BACK TO THE NEW NORMAL

How do you handle getting back to some semblance of normal after a day like Dexter and Melinda just had? Neither of them was really sure. The first order of business for Monday would be to have the ring resized. Dexter had figured that his little finger was about the same size as Melinda's ring finger. Wrong! The ring was so loose she was afraid to wear it because she might lose it. So, she put tape around it so it wouldn't fall off.

Sunday dawned, and the Middleton family headed off to the Mercy and Grace Christian Church on the outskirts of Coral. Dexter went over to pick up Melinda. She nearly always joined the Middletons for church and then lunch afterward.

Melinda's mother had died of cancer. Melinda was only 12 when she lost her Mom. Reuben Miller, Melinda's dad, completely fell apart and started drinking heavily. He lost his job and, if Dexter's dad hadn't helped him out by signing up local farmers to lease his land, he would have lost everything. Mr. Middleton also paid the taxes on Reuben's land, although Reuben never knew that.

As a result of all this, the Middletons had given Melinda a key to their house and told her that, if she ever needed it, she could stay in their guest room any time and as long as she wanted. She only took advantage of the offer a few times., Except when her dad was on one of his binges, she stayed home to take care of him. But she spent a lot of time with Dexter and the Middletons. Mrs. Middleton had become almost a pseudo-mother to Melinda.

On the car ride to church, Dexter confirmed with Melinda that they should ask Pastor Grayson if he would perform the wedding ceremonies. "And I am thinking we could have the wedding at the Ranch!" said Melinda. "We spend an awful lot of time there and it is a beautiful setting!"

"As I said before, you get to choose all those details." reiterated Dexter. "But I'll help any way I can."

Soon they arrived at the church. Mercy and Grace Christian Church had originally been two separate churches. Mercy Bible Church and Grace Christian Church each had very small buildings and very small congregations so, about ten years previously, they had merged into one church. They had still been very small, until they installed Pastor Emil Grayson to replace the old pastor who retired about five years ago. Pastor Grayson was fairly young, and an extremely dynamic speaker. Everybody loved him, and Mercy and Grace Christian Church had grown to be the largest church in Coral and even had a number of members from nearby towns. They were getting so large that soon they would need a bigger building,

As Melinda and Dexter entered the sanctuary, Pastor Grayson congratulated them and pointed out where the rest of the Middleton family was sitting.

"I guess word gets around!" said Dexter. Could we see you for a few minutes after the service?"

"Certainly!" answered Pastor Grayson.

After the service was over everybody sang "Onward Christian Soldiers!" which was one of the pastor's favorites.

Pastor took them into his "office" which consisted of a couple of chairs, a big desk and a small table with a copy machine. On the desk was a phone and a laptop computer.

"Now, what can I do for you? asked Pastor.

"Well, we would really like to have you marry us!" said Melinda. "We are thinking of a date shortly after school is out and I'd like to have it at the Ranch, if you know about that."

"I've been out there a few times and even conducted a wedding there a couple of years ago. It's a beautiful place for a wedding, as long as the weather is good. Sure, I'd be honored to do that!" responded Pastor Grayson. "A few years ago I even put together a little pre-wedding mini-seminar I call "Hopefully Happily Ever After." It can point out some of the adjustments and compromises each of you have to make to maintain a giving and forgiving relationship. It takes about an hour and I highly recommend it. Just let me know if and when you would be interested."

"By the way, Dexter, I saw your Traci Movement Parade and I applaud your efforts. 'Try Respect and Compassion Instead' and 'Love your neighbor, Forgive 70 times seven, Let he who is without sin cast the first stone, and Judge not lest you be judged' are powerful and life changing biblical messages. If there is anything I can do to help, count me in. I hope you will have it again next year. And if you would like to give the congregation a talk about your efforts just let me know."

"That would be fantastic!" exclaimed Dexter. "Give me a couple of weeks to put a presentation together. Is it ok if I bring Anthony along? He's helped me a lot. I know your congregation here is almost all white but..."

Pastor cut him off. "Our congregation is almost all white only because Coral is almost all white. There is no other reason! I have met with the Davis family that just recently moved to town and I think they will be attending soon and hopefully become members. If anybody leaves because they join, then I am not getting my...or your...or God's message across!"

"Amen, pastor!" Said Dexter. There was nothing else to be said but Amen. Dexter and Melinda thanked Pastor Grayson, then set off to meet the rest of the Middleton family at the Coral Steak House for lunch.

CHAPTER 17
THE TRUMBLE GAME

Right after football practice Monday afternoon Dexter and Melinda headed to the jewelers to have the ring resized. They would have to leave it there for a few days, much to Melinda's chagrin. All day long practically every girl in school just had to see the ring and Melinda was more than happy to show it to them. Everybody wished the two of them well. Without the ring, even for a few days, people might think they had broken up already. Plus, Melinda really liked the diamond ring, even with all the tape on it to keep it from falling off her ring finger. However, they would just have to manage for a day or two.

As the little car with Melinda driving pulled into the Ranch driveway, Dexter commented, "I think we need to get you a bigger car."

"Why?" asked Melanie.

"Because I barely fit in this one!" complained Dexter. "We'll get you an SUV like mine and there will be lots more room."

"But I like my little car!" Asserted Melanie emphatically. "Besides, it is the only thing my dad ever actually gave me."

Dexter was afraid this might develop into an argument. And the last thing he wanted was to get into an argument with his soon-to-become bride. "Ok!" he said. "But if the seat breaks, we get you a new, or at least newer SUV. Deal?" he asked.

"Deal!" she said.

Practices were getting better all the time. In the high scoring game against Clifford Lake, Wayde had passed for over 200 yards, had run for another 50 yards, and was responsible for three touchdowns with no turnovers. For that, he was awarded the conference player of the week. Dexter and Lindy were named co-defensive players of the week. For Dexter this was a fairly normal occurrence. But for Lindy and Wayde, this was a first. For Coach it meant that Coral really did know how to play football and was no longer the conference doormat.

The Trumble Toros were Coral's next opponent. And it was at Coral. The Toros came into the game with a 3-2 record and had a running back who, while he wasn't particularly fast, was built like a tank. His name was Lewis Hedge, and he was about 6' 1" tall and weighed about 215 pounds. Last year Trumble triple-teamed Dexter for almost the entire game, with Hedge running for over 150 yards in a 30-7 runaway Trumble win. But that was last year. The Coral game plan was basically the same as for Clifford Lake. A solid running game with Wayde's sharp passes, both short and, whenever possible, deep slants and crossing patterns.

This was a Saturday afternoon game and once again it was a really good Autumn day for football. Temperature about 75 degrees with a wind at about 10 to 15 miles an hour. That might make the deep passing game a bit more difficult, especially when throwing into the wind.

When all the exercises and drills were done and the National Anthem was sung by both teams' choirs, as usual, it was time for the coin flip. Dexter called "tails" as always. This time it WAS tails. Coach chose to receive. They would be going into that 15 mph wind. That wind carried the opening kick all the way into the end zone. A couple of running plays behind Dexter and Lindy yielded a first down, and a short slant pass from Wayde to Red got the Lancers out to the 50 yard line. Methodically, Wayde guided the team downfield to a touchdown. Elston's point after quickly made it 7-0 Coral. His ensuing kickoff was unusually short with the high wind, and the Toros ran it back almost to their own 45 yard line. The Toros' coach called for triple-teaming Dexter and Lewis ran right into the arms of Lindy for only a one yard gain. Second and ten. Same play but there was no hole for Lewis to run through and he actually lost a yard. A third down pass was almost picked off by Ralph Jackson. On fourth and ten, Trumble punted and, with the stiff wind helping, the ball went out of bounds at the Coral two yard line.

On first down Wayde faked a handoff into the middle of the Toros' line, then ran fifty-five yards down the left sideline all the way to the Trumble 43. With Dexter and Lindy opening big holes right in the middle of the defensive line and alternating between Red and Kenny running, it took a while but Coral found the end zone again. 14 - 0Coral.

Offensively, the Toros' coach tried bringing the tight end in, along with the linemen he already had triple teaming Dexter and effectively double teaming Lindy. Still Lindy and Dexter jammed up the entire middle. The first quarter ended with the score still Coral 14 Trumble 0. Lewis Hedge had four carries for one yard. The Trumble coach was beginning to sense it was going to be a long afternoon.

Coach Gayton could tell, however, that fighting through those double and triple teams was really tiring out both Dexter and Lindy. He would need to give them each a break, even though they had only played one quarter. First he took Lindy out for about the first four offensive plays, then Dexter for about four plays. The Coral running game wasn't nearly as effective, but Wayde kept completing third down passes for first downs. Eventually Coral scored again to give the Lancers a 21-0 lead. Coach put both Lindy and Dexter back in for defense and, although the Toros did get a couple of first downs, they never evencrossed midfield. By halftime Coral had added a field goal and Coral led 24 - 0.

The Toros' Coach came out throwing in the second half. While Lindy and Dexter could almost completely clog up the middle of the Toros' line, they could not get near the quarterback. Completing mostly five to ten yard passes Trumble managed to get to the Coral 15 yard line where, on fourth and eight, they had to settle for a field goal. Still, 24 - 3, Coral. The Lancers went back to their running game, also running as much time off the clock as possible. Again, it took some time but they eventually ended up in the end zone again and led 31-3 at the end of quarter number three.

The fourth quarter saw Trumble again rely on their passing game. They worked the ball all the way down to the Coral eight yard line but, on the next play, Elston intercepted a slightly underthrown pass. Coach Gayton decided it was a safe enough lead that he could bring in his substitutes. He was pleasantly surprised first, when the Trumble Coach also sent in his subs, and second, when the Coral subs, although they did give up a touchdown, also scored one of their own with the final score climbing to 38-10 in favor of Coral.

After starting the season with three consecutive losses, Coral was now three and three for the year. "Maybe a New streak" thought Coach Gayton. "This time a positive one."

CHAPTER 18
JUST OUR LUCK

Dexter and Melinda had retrieved the resized engagement ring and the interlocking wedding ring. They agreed to keep the wedding ring at the Middleton's house until the wedding. Dexter had asked Anthony to be his best man and he was happy to accept. They had just about decided on a date. They would graduate on the last Friday in May and the wedding rehearsal would be the next evening with the wedding on Sunday afternoon. The wedding would be set for the Ranch with the Mercy and Grace Christian Church basement as a backup plan in case of bad weather. In addition to Anthony as best man, Dexter chose Lindy and Wayde as groomsmen. Melinda's best friend Sarah Stallings would be her Maid of Honor and Shelly, Sarah's one year younger sister, would be a bridesmaid. She hadn't figured out who the other bridesmaid would be, but there was plenty of time to decide.

They also had yet to pick a place for their honeymoon. Dexter liked the idea of a cruise, but his dad advised, "Son, a honeymoon is a very private time for just the two of you. You DON'T want to share it with a thousand strangers on a boat!" And Melinda agreed.

They could go on a cruise anytime. So, they hadn't actually decided on a honeymoon destination yet either.

They had met with Pastor Grayson again and gone through his "Hopefully Happily Ever After" mini seminar. They found it very helpful and it covered a lot of things they hadn't even thought about. Dexter was all set to give a fifteen minute talk on his TRACI Movement the Sunday after the Chalcedney game.

The next items on the agenda had to do with getting Melinda into Vermillion University and both of them into married student housing or, if that wasn't possible or necessary, into an off-campus apartment. She had thought there was no money for her to go to college, so she hadn't applied anywhere. Her grades and test scores were all good but there were all kinds of hoops to jump through, as Dexter had found out earlier. But Dexter had the whole athletic department to help him through. Maybe they might help her, too. He would check on that.

The week once again seemed to really speed by. Once more it seemed like they had just been playing. But this would be an away game with a long bus ride to Chalcedney, home of the Gems, 40 miles away from Coral. On the long bus trip, the morale was good. After all, they had now won three in a row. Chalcedney, like Coral, had a 3-3 record but they had just gotten their star quarterback back. He was now recovered from a serious arm injury. When he was healthy, they were undefeated. His specialty was the rollout run pass option and he was a good and fast runner with a strong arm. He would be playing big time college football somewhere next year. At least that was pretty much the consensus of all the sports writers in the area.

Chalcedney won the coin toss and elected to receive. Another mild October evening with little or no wind and just a very few clouds in the sky. Elston had a nice, high, and deep kick, but the Gem's returner made it back to their own thirty yard line. They say you can't teach speed and you can't teach height. It didn't take long to see that Chalcedney had both. Their quarterback was about 6'

4" and their receivers were all over six feet. They could reach right over the outstretched hands of the Coral defenders and catch the ball. All the quarterback had to do was throw the ball over the top of the Coral corner backs and then let them try to outrun the Coral safeties. And they did. About a half dozen completed passes and they were in the end zone. 7-0 Chalcedney.

It had only taken about four minutes for the Gems to traverse the 70 yards to the goal line. Coral took the kickoff up to their own 25. Enter Wayde and the Coral offense. A running play handoff to Red netted five yards. A quick slant pass to Elston got about eight yards for a first down. Relying mostly on running plays using Red and Kenny with quick passes thrown in as necessary. Eventually Coral worked their way to the Chalcedney eight yard line with a first down. Wayde had Kenny in motion to the right side and the quarterback handed him the ball as he went by. Kenny went almost to the right sideline before spotting Red in the end zone and firing a pass, which Red juggled and then held on to. Coral had taken a lot more time than their opponent, but they had knotted the score at seven apiece as the quarter ended. Neither Dexter nor Lindy had gotten anywhere near the Gem's quarterback, but Chalcedney hadn't gotten near Wayde either.

On the Coral kickoff, one of the Lancer players was called for holding; the runback plus the 15 yard penalty brought the ball almost to midfield. It was a very costly mistake. A handoff into the Coral line surprised the Lancers but only went for four yards. But a short slant pass netted fifteen yards and a deeper pass set up Chalcedney with a first and goal at the Coral six.

Two runs right up the middle made it third down and two. Then a beautiful fake handoff up the middle and a quick toss to the wide receiver headed down the left side toward the end zone. Elston caught up with him just short of the goal line, but the runner's momentum carried both of them into the end zone.. 14 - 7, favor of the Gems. The only scoring for the rest of the first half was done by Coral with a field goal as the half ended with Chalcedney leading

14 - 10. Coach once again knew that both Dexter and Lindy were getting worn out.

The Chalcedney coach was doubling Dexter, but he was sending different linebackers and occasionally safeties at Dexter and Lindy every time Coral was on defense. The two of them never knew where the extra blockers were coming from. This didn't help much when the Gems were passing because their quarterback got the ball off so fast. But neither Lindy nor Dexter could consistently get through the line or totally block up the running game.

If the game remained close, Coach would have to give his two big guys a rest late in the third quarter to have them rested and refreshed for the final 12 minutes or so. Would the Coral subs be up to it? Coach really hoped so.

Coral took the ball to begin the second half. Again, they marched it down the field with a good mix of runs behind Dexter and Lindy and quick but slightly deeper passes. They scored a touchdown with a nice pass to Ralph Jackson in the end zone. 17 - 14 favor of Coral. Once again they had run nearly six minutes off the clock. Elston put everything he had plus a little extra into his kickoff. It made it all the way into the end zone, so the returner settled for a touchback. A few minutes' worth of medium-deep passes and the Gems were "knocking on the door" again. A couple more runs and it was third and goal from the Coral one. A fake up the middle and a run to the left side of the formation, and they were in the end zone again, taking a 21-17 lead. Coach substituted for Lindy first, for four or five plays, and then the same for Dexter. The two teams were evenly matched and the game looked like it would be close all the way. The defenses stiffened and the teams traded punts several times as the third quarter ended with no more scoring.

Nobody could mount a drive for most of the final quarter. With about five minutes left, Coral got the ball after a short Gems' punt with excellent field position at the Chalcedney 41 yard line. On a called pass. Wayde couldn't find anybody open, so he ran all the way to the Chalcedney four yard line. Two runs up the middle and

Coral reclaimed the lead at 24 to 21 with two and a half minutes left in regulation. The Gems quarterback answered by driving 75 yards with a series of very quick 15 to 20 yard precision passes, all down the sidelines so his receivers could get out of bounds and stop the clock. Now it was 28-24 in favor of Chalcedney, with a minute and a half left.

Wayde wasn't done either. He skillfully guided the team down to a first and goal at the Gems' three yard line. The first play was a run that actually lost a yard as the ball carrier was knocked back into Wayde and Wayde didn't get up. Time out with fifteen seconds left. Wayde was helped off the field. Kenny Turner took over as quarterback. Second and four. Both teams were out of time outs. If they did it right, Coral could get at least two plays in. If they ran the ball and didn't make it time would run out. If they didn't make it but got out of bounds, they could get another play and kick a tying field goal. Coach called another fake into the line and a run toward the left sideline. If Kenny could find Elston open throw the pass. If not, get out of bounds or throw the ball away, and they would go for the field goal. Kenny saw Elston wide open in the back of the end zone. But, although Wayde had tried to teach him how to grip the ball differently, for a better spiral, in the heat of the moment Kenny forgot all that. He threw one of his "flutter balls," which wobbled badly and fell 15 feet short of Elston and right into the arms of the Gems defender for the interception. Game over. 28-24 Chalcedney.

And, on top of that, Wayde was injured. Coach's worst fears were realized. Fortunately, that turned out to be just a bruise. Not too serious. And it looked like he should be ok after a week of rest and some time in a whirlpool.

The first one to hurry out to see Kenny Turner, even if he was somewhat hobbled with the bruised leg, was Wayde. Kenny was still lying on the turf, in tears, and saying over and over "He was open, he was open!" Wade did his best to console Kenny. Soon the whole team was gathered around Kenny. "I'm so sorry guys," said Kenny through the tears. "I let everybody down! Wayde, you would have made that throw easily and we would have won!"

Just then Coach joined the group. "Guys," he said loud enough for everybody to hear. "That is just as much my fault as anybody's. I called that play to the left sideline, which meant Kenny had to throw across his body. That is tough enough normally, but to come in without even a chance for a few practice throws made it doubly difficult. I should have at least called the play to the right side. If we have to blame somebody, blame me."

"We are not blaming anybody." stated Dexter. "We win as a team and we lose as a team. Period!"

Most of the long bus ride was quiet. Near the end of the trip, Dexter said to no one in particular, "You know we already beat the Shady Elm Owls and the Clifford Lake Hawks. And now we play the Fall City Falcons. How about if we have as our theme to 'Beat all the Birds?' What do you think?" Nobody objected and most of the team thought it was a great idea. The rest of the trip was back to the normal conversations and discussions.

"Once again, Dexter sure knows how to break the tension." thought Coach Gayton.

CHAPTER 19
LOOSE ENDS

On Sunday morning after breakfast Dexter headed over to Melinda's house to pick her up for church. Dexter had his notes for his 15 minute talk about the TRACI Movement. With both of them in the car, they had a little time to talk. "I checked with the athletic department at Vermillion and they gave me a list of everything we have to do." began Dexter. There is one more test we both have to take, and we can take the trip over to the school in the spring. We can make a day of it. They are sending us the application forms, and we can fill them out online. We can check out the housing situation at the same time. But I am a little worried about one thing. I know you love animals. But am I pushing you too hard to go to Vet school? If you would rather, you could become a Vet Assistant, or you could be a business major, or whatever you want. I want you to be my partner as well as my wife. And we both start with four years of kind of general pre-vet education to get our bachelors' degrees, so we have some time to decide."

"I'm still kind of in shock from everything." Melinda said thoughtfully. "I do love animals and the vet thing is an exciting opportunity. The main drawback is when you can't save an animal and you have to face the farmer or the pet owner. But yes, after thinking about it for over a week now, I would like that!"

"Dad told me he had the exact same feelings years ago, and it never goes entirely away. But you do get sort of used to it and, if you do the job right, there will be a whole lot of successes and very few failures."

Dexter pulled the car into the church parking lot and they went in. Anthony was already there, chatting with Pastor Grayson and the rest of the Middleton family, who had saved three seats for them. The church service started with announcements and a hymn, "Great Is Thy Faithfulness," which was one of Dexter's favorites.

Then pastor introduced both Dexter and Anthony and said they would tell the congregation a little about Dexter's new endeavor "The TRACI Movement." Dexter began, "About a year ago, after a football game in Salem, I met someone. His team had just stomped us and he scored three touchdowns against us. And I wanted to congratulate him. We were, and still are, two very different people. He's black and I am white. He can practically outrun a gazelle and I can't outrun much. He has a slender physique and no one would ever use that term when describing me." The congregation laughed.

Dexter continued. "We found out that we actually did have a lot in common. We both wanted to give back to our communities. He had his ideas and I had mine. We decided to get together for coffee to meet at The Ranch. And we did. We found that we were both trying to end all the racial hatred in the area. We became best friends. Even though his team not only beat us again this year, but he scored two touchdowns and set up the winning field goal to beat us almost single- handedly. I'll let Anthony tell you about his projects and then I'll tell you about mine. Maybe our two churches could even work together. Ladies and gentlemen, let me introduce my best friend and soon to be the best man in our wedding, Anthony Thuley!" There was an enthusiastic round of applause.

Anthony talked to the congregation about differences. The gang problems and drug problems that they faced in Salem. How he and the entire team had found some available land and made it into a food garden and were donating all the food to needy families. And they were trying to fix up and refurbish an old local building to set up a basketball league to try to counter the appeal of gangs. He closed his part by mentioning the get-together at The Ranch between the two football teams and how much fun they all had. He referenced the TRACI parade, then he thanked everyone, particularly the Pastor, for the opportunity to speak, and turned the microphone back to Dexter.

Dexter began with "A while back a large city that shall remain nameless decided to do something to eliminate all car accidents. So they did. After that they were all to be called 'crashes.' We have been told by all the political-correctness people that if we just call it a 'chair' or 'chair person' we will make the term gender neutral and all the problems will magically go away. Just like the way they eliminated all accidents. Talk is cheap, but talk without deeds is pretty much worthless. I wrote a poem about it and I'd like to read it to you if I may. It uses a term from a long time ago and a long-forgotten Vice President. It's called 'Ode to the Political Correctness People.'"

Dexter took out a sheet of paper.

> "To the effete corps of impudent snobs
> who gave us political correctness,
> if you really believed all that stuff you espouse
> you would not so much disrespect us!
> Who gave you the right to tell the rest of us
> just what we all should be thinking,
> where we should go and what we should do
> and what water we all should be drinking.
> Clean up your act before preaching to us.
> Better yet tell us you were just joking.
> Mind your own business, leave us alone,
> and go back to whatever it was you were smoking!"

That brought some chuckles from the congregation along with a number of "Amens!" Dexter finished by stating some of the goals of his "movement" and what TRACI stood for.

There was an enthusiastic applause when he was finished. When the service was over, a number of people came up to him to wish him well and asked how they could help. He took down lots of names and numbers. Pastor had said he could have a free will offering either this Sunday or next, but Dexter said he had been selling tee shirts with the poem on the front and the TRACI logo on the back and he was raising enough money from the shirts. But he thanked Pastor again for letting him and Anthony speak. Pastor Grayson asked Anthony for the name and phone number of the pastor of his church. All three thought it would be really great if the two churches could work together.

Dexter invited Pastor and Anthony to join his family for lunch but they both had prior commitments. They each asked for a "rain check."

CHAPTER 20

LIFE AND DEATH AND A BEAUTIFUL BOWL

When it came time for Monday practice Coach was nowhere to be seen. Instead, it was just Paul Horn and Thad Hollaway, the two coordinators, who ran practice.

Paul told the team to gather up. "Coach isn't here today!" he said somberly. "Unfortunately his mother has been in the hospital for several weeks and she passed away yesterday. He has to make all the funeral arrangements and won't be back until later in the week. So, you are stuck with us for a couple of days. The game plan will be much the same as last week. Coach wants Wayde to rest his bruised leg and spend some time in a whirlpool. Since we don't have a whirlpool, he made arrangements to use the one at the YMCA in Coral. Ken Turner will practice running the offense until later in the week. Now let's get started with our usual routine!"

By now, everybody knew the procedure. The next game up was Coral's last home game of the season. Last week's last-second loss gave the Lancers a 3-4 record. Their opponent, the Fall City Falcons, were also 3-4. And there was a great deal at stake for both teams. It required a winning record to get into the end-of-the-season state tournament. Whichever team lost would be eliminated. Even if Coral won, they still had to contend with undefeated Windham, a school about four times as big as Coral, and currently rated number two in Class 5. The odds were already figured for the game and the Lancers would be 28 point underdogs. But that was next week. This week, the focus would be entirely on Fall City.

There was only one funeral home in Coral and it was called "Peaceful Valley Funeral Home." And only one cemetery on the outskirts of town had the same name and was owned by the same people. Coach's Mother had been fine on Sunday morning in the hospital and plans were to bring her home the next day. But she fell asleep shortly after the Gaytons left the hospital and never woke up. She was in her late 80s and the doctors listed her cause of death as old age. Coach and his family were devastated. And it happened just when they thought she would be coming home. Coach made the arrangements while fighting back tears. The funeral home had two rooms, one held up to 75 people upstairs, the other held up to 300 and was downstairs. Coral had very few funerals where more than 300 would be attending. Nearly all of his mom's friends had passed away, so he selected the smaller venue. If they were lucky, there might be a dozen guests so the attendance would undoubtedly be small. Coach had found Pastor Grayson who agreed to officiate. The funeral was set for Thursday evening.

Little by little, Wayde and Kenny had become friends. And when Kenny was so despondent after his pass was intercepted, it was Wayde who hobbled over on his bruised leg and helped him up and comforted him. After that devastating loss, Wayde invited Kenny over to his house for an after-game snack and some encouragement. Kenny stared at a beautiful wooden bowl on the mantle by the fireplace. "Did you make that?" asked Kenny.

"No, my dad makes those. He says woodworking, especially making bowls, is his way of relaxing. He's got some equipment in the basement," answered Wayde. "The whole basement is full of bowls."

"Well, my dad owns the hardware store and he has all the latest woodworking equipment and his bowls don't look nearly as good as that," admired Kenny. "Could I take this and show it to him?"

"Sure." replied Wayde.

An hour or so later Kenny was at home showing his dad the remarkable bowl. "What kind of lathe does he have that he can turn bowls like that?" asked Mr. Turner. "<u>That</u> is really something special!"

After dinner Ken's dad got the number from his son and called Wayde's dad about the bowl. "We have a group of woodworkers with varying degrees of expertise. We meet every Wednesday evening. If you are interested, we'd like to have you show us how it's done."

"Well," said Mr. Davis, "it's just a hobby and about all I do so far is bowls, so maybe I might attend some time to learn about other kinds of woodworking if that would be ok."

"Sure!" said Mr. Turner. "We have all the latest equipment and books and woodworking magazines. 8:00 pm every Wednesday including tonight. We'll look forward to meeting you!"

On his way to the hardware store for the first time, Mr. Davis wondered what kind of reception he would get as probably the first African American to join the group. He needn't have worried. It wasn't a very large group but they greeted him warmly and everyone wanted to know how he made such great bowls.

On Thursday evening Coach and his wife headed over to the funeral home. Her parents were out of town so it just might be that she and Coach and their daughters and their families would be the only ones there. It was a sad realization that all of his mom's friends had already passed away. Coach and Mrs. Gayton arrived at 6:30 and the funeral was to start at 7:00. The Gaytons' three daughters and their families arrived soon after. All the Gaytons would have formed a greeting line but there was no one to greet. Coach had put together a lot of pictures of prominent events in his mother's life and there was a great deal of reminiscing.

At 6:55 a few cars pulled into the lot and within minutes the parking lot started filling. In walked Dexter and Melinda, followed by the entire football team and the two assistant coaches. Coach had to wipe away the tears. "You didn't have to do that!" he said as he shook hands and hugged everyone. "But I really appreciate it."

"We're all family!" said Dexter, "And we wanted to be here for you. That's what family does." Everybody was appropriately reserved for the actual funeral ceremony and on the trip to the cemetery and the mini-ceremony there. Even the always upbeat Dexter was quiet and somber, as was Melinda. It was the first time Coach had seen the team in suits.

After everything was finished, Coach thanked them again and apologized for not having a meal after the funeral, explaining that they didn't know anyone was coming. "How did you even know where and when it was?" he asked Dexter, who he suspected was the orchestrator.

"Well," explained Dexter, "this is the only funeral home in Coral so I just called them and got the information. When I told the whole team, every single player and both assistants wanted to attend. Until we got here, we didn't know we would be the only non-family ones here but that is fine. And we all ate dinner before coming so nobody needs food anyway. We are so sorry for your loss." And everyone headed home.

After being quiet most of the trip back to their house Coach said, "You know, Mom would have loved the way this all turned out." Mrs. Gayton agreed.

CHAPTER 21
BEAT ALL THE BIRDS

Coach Gayton was back at practice on Friday. Coaches Horn and Holloway had done a good job in his absence but, since it was the last home game of the season, it was also a day to honor all the soon-to-graduate Seniors. Those honors, as well as final preparations for the Fall City Falcons, made for a very busy day.

The Falcons had a quarterback who was a pretty decent passer and a pretty good runner, but not really great at either. They had a couple of fair but not really good wide receivers and an adequate running back. However, they did excel on defense and were ranked second defensively in the conference behind only Windham. If Wayde's bruised ankle was ok and he could play, Coach was confident the Lancers could win. Wayne said his leg felt fine so Coach let him practice. Coach tweaked the game plan just a bit. Coral would mainly use the ground game for at least the first quarter with only an occasional pass, if they could catch the Falcon defense off-guard. The second quarter would be more of the same as long as it was working. In the third quarter Coral would switch to the passing game, including some longer ones. If the game plan was working and Coral had a sizeable lead, the substitutes would play most of the fourth quarter, with mostly runs to use up the clock. Wayde was only supposed to run if it was absolutely necessary and take it easy on his bruised leg.

Coach thought practice went well. He was feeling closer to this team than any he had previously coached. Everybody, including the subs, gave everything they had on every play. Coach never liked the terms 110%. If you really gave 100%, you couldn't have anything left, not even an extra 10%. Coach couldn't ask for more.

The game would be an evening game and, on a mid-October day, it was a little on the chilly side with just a light breeze. Before the actual start of the game all the seniors on the football team plus all the cheer leaders lined up in the center of the field. Coach took the microphone and, starting with the bench players and working his way up to the three Senior co-captains, Dexter, Lindy, and Wayde, he had something nice to say about each player. Then he turned the microphone over to the cheerleader coach who did the same thing. The ceremonies ended with cheers for everyone.

As always, Dexter called tails; this time he won the coin toss. Coach chose to kick off. Dexter had talked up the "Beat All the Birds" theme and there were signs all through the stands with that message. The game turned out to be a sell-out and this time nearly all the fans were noisily supporting the Lancers. "What a difference a few wins can make!" thought Coach.

Elston's kickoff almost made the end zone, with help from the wind, and the Falcon kick returner got back to the Fall Creek 21 yard line. Two hand-offs into the middle of the Lancer line yielded only a yard. On third and 11, the Falcon quarterback intended to pass, but Dexter broke through the line and tackled him for a ten yard loss. On fourth down and 21, the Falcons punter kicked it high and deep and Elston had to make a fair catch at the Coral 39. Following the script, Wayde alternated between Red and Kenny, each in turn running through big holes opened by both Dexter and Lindy for substantial gains. Ten running plays netted the 61 yards into the zone and Coral led 7-0.

Elston's second kickoff made it to the Fall City ten yard line and was run back to their 27. The Falcon's coach switched to his quick, short passing game and got a couple of first downs. Facing a third down and six from the Coral 43, the pass was complete, but the receiver only gained four yards. The Falcon's coach thought briefly about going for the first down but decided to punt instead. The punt went out of bounds at the Coral five yard line. Again, sticking with the running game, Wayde and the team maneuvered their way steadily down the field. Coral faced one fourth down and one yard to go from the Falcon 35 yard line. Dexter managed to move the whole pile ten yards down the field as Kenny easily ran for the first down. The lengthy 95 yard drive gave Coral a 14 - 0 lead and used up the rest of the first quarter.

Switching sides, and now kicking against the wind, Elston still managed to get the kickoff all the way into the end zone so the ball came out to the Falcon 25.

The Falcon coach had another "trick up his sleeve." He put into his lineup a bench player named Joe Treadwell who was their biggest substitute at 6' 2" and about 245 pounds. They put him in motion-timing the play just right so, when the ball was snapped, he was going full speed right at Dexter. Along with the regular lineman, Dexter was being hit by two or three players. It was definitely taking Dexter out of the play. Sometimes Lindy broke through to get at their quarterback, but not very often. Suddenly the Falcons had the time to run or pass as they willed. They worked their way steadily down the field to a first and goal at the Lancer eight yard line. Treadwell again smashed head on into Dexter and both went down. Only Dexter got up. They had to cart poor Joe off the field. Deemed a concussion, he would be all right but done for the day. The play had made it second and goal from the Coral three, a gain of five yards. A handoff into the line, without as much help blocking Dexter yielded no gain. Third down and goal found Dexter and Lindy both chasing the Falcon quarterback and bringing him down back at the Coral 16. A Falcon 33 yard field goal made it Lancers 14 Falcons 3.

The Falcons kickoff into the wind was high but short and Elston fair caught it at the Coral 32. Coach made sure Dexter was okay, but after the beating he had taken, he put Red in and kept Dexter on the bench for the rest of the first half. Without the big guy in the game, the Coral offense wasn't nearly as efficient and only mustered a field goal for the rest of the half. But the Falcons couldn't move the ball consistently either, and that left the halftime score 17 - 3, Coral with the fourteen point lead.

In the second half the Lancers wanted to work on their passing game. Coach knew that with the Windham game next week Coral would have to be able to pass consistently to have any chance at all. Plus, a two-touchdown lead is not, nor ever will be, insurmountable. Coral had already lost several games in which they had two touchdown leads.

Fall City kicked off again, and again it was high and, into the wind which had picked up a bit. He still got off a good kick which Elston took to his own 25 yard line First and ten. Dexter was back in the lineup and fairly well rested. He and Lindy were able to block up the middle on passing plays but the Falcon coach was blitzing his corner-backs and his safeties in no particular order from the outside of the formation. Wayde only had a few seconds to find somebody open and throw the ball or just throw it away. After finding his brother open and connecting on several nice passes, Wayde faced a third down and six from the Falcon 26. Nobody was open and he was just about to throw the ball away when he saw some "daylight.". He dashed down the left sideline for a nice 11 yard gain and then deftly stepped out of bounds. Coach held his breath for a minute, then relaxed when Wayde stepped out. First and ten at the Falcon 15. After a throwaway pass on first down, on second and ten Wayde saw his tight end, Ralph Jackson, open at the three yard line and his pass led Ralph right into the end zone. "Perfectly done!" thought Coach Gayton" The PAT made it a 24 - 3 lead for Coral. The 75 yard 18 play drive had taken some time off the clock and there were only a couple of minutes left in the quarter. Coach took both Dexter and Lindy out for a rest and their substitutes held their own as the quarter ended.

Coach made the decision to rest Wayde, Elston, Dexter, and Lindy for the rest of the game unless the game started to get close again. Fall City did march right down the field a couple of times but a 15 yard holding penalty stopped one drive, a Roger Morrison interception stopped another, and the third ended with a fourth down and eight field goal.

Coral, on the other hand, was moving the ball fairly well with Kenny at quarterback and Red still in at running back. On one drive they had to settle for a 35 yard Elston field goal and, on the final drive of the game, with all substitutes in the game for both sides, Kenny hit a wide open Red with a nice 15 yard pass for a touchdown and a final score of 34 - 6. They had "Beaten All the Birds!"

CHAPTER 22
THE WINDHAM GAME

The players that were on the team last year, although there weren't a lot of them, recalled the 51 - 3 final score. The Lancers were now four and four for the season and had actually won four of their last five games. They were a much-improved team. Were they improved enough to compete with Windham? They would find out soon enough.

Practices went well all week. The weather forecast was a different story. Thursday and Friday were supposed to be in the 80's for high temperatures. Then a cold front was supposed to come through Saturday night with temperatures dropping into the forties with severe thunderstorms, high winds,and even tornados possible. The Windham coach called Coach Gayton to say they wanted to move the game from a 6:00 pm start to a noon or maybe 1:00 pm start to beat the storm. Coach Gayton agreed and they settled on a start at noon. The state had mandated a number of years ago that, in the event of nearby lightning, the game must be suspended to be completed at a later date if possible. Otherwise, whatever the score was at the time it was suspended would be considered the final score. Also, because the State tournament would start the following weekend, any tie in regulation was not going to be resumed.

Windham had excellent offensive and defensive lines, an all-state quality quarterback, and really fast wide receivers. Their defense, this year wasn't quite up to their normal standards but the offense was so good, so far at least, their weak defense hadn't hurt them. Their only close game had been a non-conference match-up and they still won by two touchdowns in a 45 - 31 shoot-out. Keeping Dexter and Lindy at least reasonably well rested would be a priority. The Coral subs had been holding their own against the rest of the conference teams, but against Windham they would be battling against linemen who outweighed them by 40 to 50 pounds each.

It took the buses almost an hour to get to the Warriors stadium. The team seemed to be loose enough, and Dexter was his usual jovial self which was always a good sign. The temperature was already dropping into the seventies by the time the Senior Recognition ceremonies were over and the skies were beginning to darken. The coin toss was won by Windham and they chose to receive. Just as Elston kicked off the sound of distant thunder could be heard. The storm was coming quicker than expected. Elston's kick was high and deep right down the middle of the field but the wind caught it and pushed way over to the left sideline. The Warrior receiver caught it, gained about five yards and was pushed out of bounds at his own 21 yard line. Windham started with the running game. At first they didn't even try the middle of the line but ran everything to the outside. Using a lot of motion and misdirection, they moved steadily down the field gaining five to ten yards per run. They were quickly across mid-field and into Coral territory. They tried a couple of plays up the middle but Dexter and Lindy were up to the challenge and they netted only a couple of yards. On third down and seven from the Coral 26, the Windham quarterback faked into the line then threw a pass about 20 yards to one of his wide receivers. Elston was defending and dived trying to knock the pass down. He managed to tip the ball a bit but the receiver juggled the ball, got a good grip on it and high-stepped into the end zone. 7 to 0, Warriors. "Not the best start," thought Coach, "but lots of time left."

After a relatively high but short kick was pretty much blown out of bounds by the wind, Coral got the ball first and ten at their own 35. Wayde faked into the line then looked for a receiver. Nobody was open but he saw some running room down the left sideline and bolted for some 20 yards before stepping out of bounds to protect his leg. First down at the Warrior 45. A series of short quick passes gave Coral a first down at the Windham 15.

An end-around play set Coral up with a first and goal at the Warrior two. Two running plays behind Dexter and Lindy and Kenny tumbled into the end zone. With the PAT it was tied at seven with only a couple of minutes left in the first quarter.

On the ensuing kickoff the wind caught the ball and the Windham returner fumbled and had to fall on it on his own 21 yard line. The wind was really blowing now and it played havoc with the long passing game. The combination of Dexter and Lindy was forcing every play wide to one side or the other and, at least so far, the corners and safeties were tackling the Windham ball carriers for short gains. The Warriors had to punt and Coral got the ball where it rolled dead at their own 35 as the quarter ended. Dexter complained he was being held on just about every offensive play. The opposing lineman would go to the ground and try to grab Dexter by his shirt and pull him down. Coach had looked closely on several plays and, although he didn't have the best vantage point, he could see that Dexter was being held on almost every play. Coach complained to the referees but to no avail. As Coral began the second quarter and the holding continued Coach could see that Dexter was getting more and more frustrated. On one play Dexter actually picked up the opposing lineman and threw him to the ground. Flags came out and Dexter was penalized 15 yards for unnecessary roughness. That stopped the Coral drive. Coach reluctantly pulled Dexter out of the lineup, first for the Coral punt, then for the defense. That would let Dexter cool off a bit and give him some rest as well. With Dexter out for several plays, Windham was able to run the ball. Lindy was now being double-blocked and the Warriors were gaining chunks of yardage right up the middle of the Coral defense. With Windham having a first and goal from the Lancer eight yard line, Coach sent Dexter back in. Windham pulled off a double reverse and scored anyway. 14 - 7, Warriors.

With the wind blowing from his left to right, the Warriors' kicker tried to aim the ball well to the left but over did it and it went out of bounds. Coach took Lindy out for a rest and, without the teamwork the two Coral linemen had developed, Coral could only net a couple of first downs before having to punt again.

With Lindy back in the game, Windham didn't get much going either and the half ended still 14 - 7.

In the Coral locker room Coach told his team that they were still very much in the game and how proud he was of them. He also made several adjustments. Since the wind now was really strong, it basically eliminated the long pass. Anything longer then fifteen yards got grabbed by the gusts, now up to 35 miles an hour. So, on defense, Coach pulled his corners and safeties up close to the line of scrimmage. That would prove to be a very good move but it was a gamble. With the entire defense close to the line of scrimmage, if anybody broke through the line and Elston or Ralph couldn't catch them, it would be a quick touchdown.

Coral received the kickoff which once again blew out of bounds. On first down, the Warrior lineman who had been holding Dexter all afternoon tried it again. This time Dexter tried a spin move and the Warrior lineman got his hand wrapped up in Dexter's shirt while Dexter dragged him several yards as he and Lindy opened a huge hole that Kenny ran through for a thirty yard run. With the Warrior lineman lying on the ground with his hand twisted up in Dexter's shirt, the officials finally acknowledged holding and tacked on another 15 yards, taking the ball all the way down to the Windham 30. "I'll be watching for that now!" said the line judge apologetically. The Windham lineman had to leave the game with a sprained wrist. A couple more running plays moved Coral down to a first down at the Warrior 16. Wayde fired a laser-like pass to his brother in the end zone to tie the game at 14 all.

The weather was getting worse by minute. First a light rain, then heavier. With the wind and the rain, the playing conditions were rapidly worsening. With the teams going nowhere, the third quarter ended still tied. The fourth quarter began with a big break for Windham. After a decent punt and Elston trying to stay away and let the ball die, he slipped in the slick mess the field was becoming and slid right into the ball. The wet and muddy football was then recovered by the Warriors all the way down at the Coral 12. With neither Dexter nor Lindy able to keep their footing, although it took four plays to get a first down and three more to get the touchdown, Windham finally got into the end zone. 21 - 14 Windham.

The teams traded punts several times. With the poor conditions, each punt and each play was an adventure. Coach wanted to give Dexter and Lindy a break but they each said they were fine and begged to stay in to the end. With about two minutes to go in regulation, Coral got the ball on their own 38 yard line, courtesy of a short punt. The field was really getting torn up and there were puddles everywhere. The officials were doing everything they could to keep the ball dry but nothing worked. Wayde ran the ball about five times in a row and got good yardage each time. He would run down whichever sideline looked most promising. Eventually Coral made it all the way to a first down at the Windham 12. Coach called the play with eight seconds left. It was to be a motion right, fake handoff and run down the left sideline. But Wayde's fake was so good, the entire Warrior defense tackled the motion man, Wayde walked into the end zone as time expired. The PAT would decide the game. Coach decided to go for two points and the win. There was a better chance to run it in anyway with these conditions. Coach called a simple quarterback sneak off another fake to a man in motion. Wayde fought his way into the end zone but suddenly there was a flag. "False start! Five yard penalty." said the back judge.

Coach called a sweep left with Kenny carrying the ball and

Wayde leading the play down the left sideline. The play worked to perfection. However, the back judge called another false start taking the ball back to the 13. Coach called the team over.

"I don't know what is going on" he said. "Let's do the same play to the other side."

Again they made it into the end zone. Once again the back judge threw another flag. "Holding" was the call this time. 15 yards took the ball all the way back to the 28 yard line. As the wind howled and the rain came down harder and the thunder was getting closer, someone handed coach a phone and a note. Coach called time out and took a look at the phone. It showed a recording of the last five or six plays. It showed clearly that no player was in motion on either of the two false start calls and no one held on the last play. The note said the kid that had been holding Dexter was the nephew of the back judge. Coach was enraged by all this. Despite the fact that Coach was in his late sixties and the back judge was probably in his forties, Coach Gayton wanted to tear the official apart. Halfway out to the field, Dexter restrained him. Elston said he thought he could kick the PAT even though it would be a 35 yard effort with a very gusty wind and rain. He would have to allow a lot for the cross wind. The ball was snapped and placed perfectly despite the conditions and Elston had just enough power behind the kick to get it there and at the last second an especially strong gust took it about three feet left of the right upright. Everyone could see it was good. The back judge started to signal no good but it was so obviously over and between the goal posts and he had to signal it "good." That would make it a 21-21 tie. But there would be no overtime because the field had become unplayable.

The storm was getting worse and everybody skipped the showers and headed for the bus. Coach found out that it was a Coral fan that had recorded those last plays; and so he was able to keep the phone and note to try to reverse the score. His team had worked too hard to be denied by a dishonest back judge.

It was a very quiet bus ride and a bit "swervy" as the wind and rain buffeted the buses but they made it back to Coral safely. But Coral, like Windham, was hard hit by the storm and the flooding and the power outages. Coach was able to make sure every one of his players had made it home safely. The storm had done major damage to a wide swath of the state and on Sunday some churches had to cancel services due to a lack of power. Including Mercy and Grace Christian Church.

CHAPTER 23
THE AFTERMATH

Sunday dawned bright and sunny, in contrast to the last evening and night. Power was still out for thousands. Many cell towers were out, so phone service was spotty. Everywhere there was the sound of chain saws cutting up branches and trees that were damaged or downed by the high winds of the night before. There was even some flooding in low areas. It would take weeks to get everything back to normal and some homes had been damaged beyond repair. The area where Coach lived was spared from the worst of the damage, although the adjacent golf course had several large ponds that weren't supposed to be there.

. After a number of failed attempts, Coach was able to get a phone call through to the Cross County Conference officials and tell them about the finish of last night's game. He was told to leave the phone with the video at the Conference's regional headquarters in Borderline and they would look at it as soon as possible. However, the Commissioner also indicated that, due to the storm damage, he was having major problems at almost every school where the playoff games were to be played. Some of the schools' facilities were underwater and it was questionable whether they could be playable by Saturday. Up to half of the games might have to be moved and all those arrangements would have to come first. Coach said he understood.

A few days later Coach was notified first that the result was changed from a tie to a Coral win by a score of 22-21, giving Coral a 5-4 record for the season. However, there was no way that, two days before the first playoff games were to be played, they could go back and change the schedule to include Coral. The commissioner apologized, and added that the back judge had been suspended and the final punishment would be determined at a later date. Coach said he understood and was fine with all that. He also made arrangements to retrieve the Coral fan's cell phone.

Early the following week, when things settled down and were at least somewhat back to normal, the Team Awards Dinner was about to begin. The athletics office had been rearranged with eight tables and eight chairs at each table and the few desks had been moved out of the way.

Coach walked briskly up to the lone microphone. First he explained that the awards ceremonies would be covered live by the local radio station.

"So behave yourselves!" he said jokingly. He began: "First I have some good news and some bad news. The good news is I was notified that, with the video evidence we gave them, the conference had changed the Windham game result to reflect a 22-21 win for Coral."

There were loud cheers and clapping.

"So, we finished the season with a 5-4 winning record!" Coach continued. "However, now the bad news. Because the Commissioner and his people were so tied up with getting all the fields lined up and repaired for this weekend's playoff games and because all of the complex scheduling had already been done for all qualifying schools but us, we won't be in the playoffs."

There was almost complete silence.

"It's not your fault but you have to understand the circumstances!" said Coach. "It couldn't be helped."

There was a bit of murmuring but everybody understood.

Coach went through some news updates. Everyone would get a Coral Varsity football letter. Including the substitutes. When called upon, they had played well and they had allowed the starters to get enough rest to be fresh for those last second efforts. They had become a very important part of the team. Coach mentioned the full ride scholarship Dexter had accepted to Vermillion University, and the fact that Melinda had gotten an academic scholarship there as well. In passing he mentioned that Dexter's friend Anthony had accepted a scholarship there also. Each part of the announcement was greeted with enthusiastic applause. Wayde and Kenny had also gotten scholarships to McNichols College so they would both be playing there next year. McNichols had a good Business Department for Kenny and a highly rated computer Science Department for Wayde. So that was all good; and every announcement brought more applause. There were a few other players with scholarships as well. Then he announced some of the awards. The Offensive Most Valuable Player was Wayde, the Defensive MVP was Dexter, the Special Teams MVP was Elston. The Most Improved player was split between Kenny and Lindy.

After a few more team awards, Coach paused, then said, "This was an exciting year for all of us. When I first came here, we had 48 guys out for the team with three more who joined us a little later. I didn't know what to expect because before I retired, I had only coached at the college level. I am sure you guys didn't know what to expect, either. The only thing we really knew was that we had a 45-game losing streak and we wanted to end it. And we did! This is the very last time we'll <u>ever</u> mention it. The applause got even louder. As the games continued, we became a really cohesive team. I think the Windham game showed that I was right...we are a GREAT team. When each of you came to my Mom's funeral, I realized how much of a family we really were. I coached for over thirty years in college, all of it at Vermillion University. My teams actually won a couple of national championships. I am as proud of you as any of those teams.

And that is saying a lot. You all have worked harder, come further, and improved more than any team I know of." Tears filled his eyes as he had everybody stand up and applaud each other. And he almost whispered, "And I love you all!"

Mrs. Farnsworth was again in her apartment doing her ironing. She had been listening to the Team Awards Dinner on her portable radio.

"They're still just a bunch of losers!" she said to herself since she was the only one there. They won a couple of games but they're still a bunch of losers." And with that she reached over and turned off the radio.